SILVERGARTH

SILVERGARTH

Sheila Spencer-Smith

CHIVERS

British Library Cataloguing in Publication Data available

This Large Print edition published by AudioGo Ltd, Bath, 2011.
Published by arrangement with the Author.

U.K. Hardcover ISBN 978 1 445 83766 6
U.K. Softcover ISBN 978 1 445 83767 3

Printed and bound in Great Britain by
MPG Books Group Limited

CHAPTER ONE

As her car topped the last hill Andrea's heart lurched at the scene ahead of her. Brackened fells met azure sky in a beauty that was breathtaking. One more bend, one more hill after this and she'd reach the turning to the cottage. Suddenly a figure loomed up at her. The windscreen darkened for a terrifying instant before she slewed the car into the bank. She was out at once, heart thudding, to bend over the hunched, rucksacked figure of a man lying, incredibly, on the road in front of her.

'I hit you!' she cried, trembling. 'Are you all right?'

To her relief he got up, unfolding himself to a massive height. The spring sunlight caught the reddish lights in his fair hair as he moved.

'Do you do that often?' he asked, hitching up the huge load on his back.

His voice was dry, but the smile he gave her reached his blue eyes with a suddenness that was magnetic. Andrea's fingers shook as she pushed her hair out of her eyes.

'What are you doing here? Where are you going?' she asked anxiously.

'Into the next world sooner than it seems.'

His voice was crisp but there was amusement in it, too.

'But this lane leads nowhere. Fell walkers use the tracks farther across. How was I to know there'd be anyone here?'

She wondered, suddenly, if he was injured after all, and looked critically at his long legs in their dark jeans. There was a patch of dirt on one side, no more, and he really did seem all right. His steady gaze was fixed on her as she raised her eyes.

'You were in the middle of the lane,' she said accusingly. 'Didn't anyone ever tell you to keep to one side facing the traffic?'

'What traffic?'

No-one looking at him as he stood there so confidently would imagine that he had been struck down by her car. She could hardly believe it herself.

'Are you really all right?' she asked more gently. 'I mean, you're not pretending?'

He laughed, his eyes crinkling at the corners in his tanned face. She saw that his mouth was wide and his teeth white.

'Pride? Not liking to be seen biting the dust? You may be right. As you say, I shouldn't have been here.'

She hadn't quite meant that, but let it pass. She could have said that she wouldn't be here either if it wasn't for Sarah's desperate telephone call this morning about the vandalising of Silvergarth House.

2

He was looking around him now, his eyes narrowed into slits as he gazed across the dale. He seemed engrossed by the splendour of it all, and she felt inexplicably touched. Once she, too, had seen beauty in everything, in sunlight on dappled, peaty water, on lichened limestone walls guarding the fields while high above, curlews wailed.

His scrutiny was so intense he seemed to have forgotten her. Worse, the car was stuck in the bank and, unlikely as it seemed, something might come round the bend at any minute.

'I can't stay here,' she said. 'Could you help me get my car free?'

He swung round and looked at it as if he'd never seen one before.

'But where are you going? Silvergarth House is back there.'

'I'm not going to Silvergarth House. In any case how did you know of it?'

He smiled down at her.

'Inside knowledge.'

Disconcerted, she stared at him. He was looking back at the view once more, apparently intrigued by the play of sunlight on stone walls. She moved towards the car. He leaped round quickly.

One moment!'

He reached the door before her and placed his hand protectively on the handle.

'Don't try moving it until we get something

3

down in front or you'll never get out of the mud. Old sacking? Anything like that in the boot?'

There was only her suitcase, and her large wooden box of paint gear. The rest of her things were on the back seat. Obviously nothing suitable there. At once he slid his arms out of the rucksack straps and wrenched off his jacket. Surely not to throw down in the mud for her car wheels to get a grip on? He must have guessed her thoughts for his lips twitched as he threw the jacket down on his rucksack. Then he leaped off the road and began tearing up handfuls of dead bracken.

'This will have to do.'

He climbed back with bronze armfuls of it. His idea worked well. Andrea backed her car into the road again with no difficulty. Gratefully she wound down her window.

'Can I give you a lift anywhere?'

He shook his head as he retrieved his jacket and put it on.

'I haven't finished reconnoitring the area on foot yet. Then I'll pick up my vehicle from where I left it this morning. There's a bit still to consider before I make up my mind about the house. We shall meet again.'

The house? Andrea narrowed his eyes. His clothes looked too good, too new for an experienced fell walker. He hauled up his rucksack and thrust his shoulders through the straps. He seemed so sure of himself, but

4

where was he going? The only house apart from Sarah's cottage was Silvergarth House, and that, in the circumstances, was out of the question.

With a brilliant smile he left. She watched him swinging effortlessly along until he turned the corner. She put the car into gear and set off. It was hard to look on it all without thinking of her sister storming off in a rage from Silvergarth six months ago. Nadine had publicly accused Sarah, their aunt's housekeeper, of dishonesty because of the change in the will which meant Sarah inherited the cottage but Sarah fully deserved her bequest. Abroad at the time of her aunt's death, she herself had been unable to stop Nadine's accusations before the damage was done.

Andrea slowed down to take the next bend and with it the turning off along the rough track that led to the cottage. She drove carefully, avoiding the ruts and looking round her at familiar sights. The cottage itself looked brooding in its tangled plot, but the door swung open as she drew up outside. She got out of the car, pausing a moment to tuck her shirt into the slim waistband of her skirt.

'You've come,' Sarah cried as she came forward to give her a hug.

Andrea was incredibly glad to see Sarah in spite of everything. She had returned from New Zealand as soon as she could but not,

5

sadly, in time for the funeral which was why Nadine, still living at Silvergarth then, had been here. Andrea was filled with deep shame at the way Sarah had been treated. Nothing had been heard of Nadine since her BBC concert series came to an end. Now Sarah lived here in the cottage alone, her husband having died a few months before.

'You'll want help with your bags,' Sarah said.

Her huge smile was welcoming as she caught hold of the handle of the suitcase as Andrea removed it from the car. They carried the luggage up the path between them and through the door into the room that was kitchen and living-room combined. On the big square table in the middle a meal was laid on a spotless cloth.

Andrea glanced round, seeing everything just as it had been in the past when she was at Silvergarth on long holidays. Often she used to call in on Sarah on her way home from an afternoon's painting up on the moors. A lump came to her throat as she remembered. It was all so much the same, blue checked curtains at the window, and a red geranium in a pot, all just as it had been when she was last here. Only Sarah was different.

Deprived of her job as companion-housekeeper on Aunt Mamie's death she had turned her talents to the holiday trade, taking summer visitors during the season. It had

6

somehow aged her. Now no-one, looking at Sarah for the first time, would believe this matronly-looking woman was only a few years older than herself. Yes, Sarah had changed and it was Nadine's doing. A thought struck Andrea.

'I met someone on the way here. Ran him down, in fact, literally. No injury thank goodness. He must be as strong as an ox.'

She gave a little laugh as if it was of no importance, but a vision of the man's piercing eyes and jutting jaw as he picked himself up and looked at her so clear it turned into a gasp.

'You don't know him? He hasn't been staying here? He seemed to know about me coming.'

Sarah poured boiling water into a brown teapot.

'Sit down, lass. You look tired. I've jacket potatoes to go with the ham salad.'

She frowned.

'There's been no-one here. Did he say what he was doing hereabouts?'

'He didn't say. He was carrying a massive rucksack. He seemed to know about Silvergarth House, though.'

Sarah put the teapot down so heavily on the table the cups rattled.

'He didn't say owt about the condition it's been left in?'

Andrea could see now that there really was

something wrong as Sarah slumped into her chair. She had always been on the stout side but now her ruddy complexion seemed paled and her hand shook a little as she poured out the tea.

'What's the matter, Sarah?' Andrea said quietly. 'You've no need to worry. Aunt Mamie left you the cottage, and nothing alters that. Of course it's not wise to let the house stand empty any longer after what's happened, but if my sister can be traced and the house sold you'll have neighbours fairly near.'

Sarah's lips tightened for a second at the mention of Nadine, but then she smiled slightly.

'Eat your tea, Andrea. Time enough for talk later.'

Nothing would budge Sarah until she was good and ready.

'What condition has the house been left in, Sarah?' Andrea said at last as she replaced her knife and fork on her plate. 'Is it very bad? Exactly what did those thugs do to it? Do the police know anything more now?'

Sarah shook her head. She put both elbows on the table and leaned forward earnestly.

'It'll be a shock when you see it for yourself, a right shock. I've not had time yet to do owt about it since the police left.'

'But how did they get in? What did they want?'

8

Andrea tried to think of her aunt's furniture, of anything other than sentimental value left in the house. Sarah gave a loud sob, and her shoulders shook. At once Andrea was at her side with her arm round her.

'Please, don't upset yourself, Sarah.'

'A fine caretaker I've been.'

'You're surely not blaming yourself. It's not your fault. How could it be? Sit down and finish your tea. I'll go across presently and see for myself. We'll leave the clearing up until tomorrow. I'd rather go on my own. I'll just need to get a sweater from my case.'

*　　　*　　　*

Prepared as she was, Andrea still felt shaken at the desolate scene that met her eyes as she unlocked the front door of Silvergarth House. Stepping across the scattered velvet curtains, her shoes scrunched on shattered ornaments from the upturned table. Coat hooks had been wrenched off the wall in a shower of plaster.

She made a move towards the door to the sitting-room. At her feet as she went in she saw one of her own watercolours smashed on the floor.

'Not the view from High Top!' she cried, throwing herself down to gather the broken pieces of frame and the torn painting.

It seemed like yesterday, that clear summer's day she had painted it, with bees murmuring in the heather. They had gone over to Martin Ackroyd's place and spent the day picnicking up on the fell top to celebrate Aunt Mamie's sixtieth birthday a few months after her parents were killed. They were all there, she, Nadine, an uncle or two and Sarah, of course. Martin had joined them for lunch with his dog, Fly. Aunt Mamie had prized this small watercolour above all others, and now it was no more.

Rushing at one of the upturned armchairs, Andrea righted it in a swift movement that had the blood rushing to her face. How dare these vandals destroy for the sake of destroying! How dare they break into this once-loved house because it now stood empty. The sofa was far too heavy for her and she tugged at it ineffectually. At last she gave up. She smoothed its cover and then lay her head against it for an instant with her long dark hair covering her face like a protecting curtain. Calmer now, she jumped up and walked to the window.

Outside, across the garden, the moors stretched to the hills. It was in her blood, this north country. She had come home. She would live and work here. She took a deep breath. The suddenness of the decision shook her. Her aunt hadn't wanted the house sold, and had hoped that one of them would choose to live in it one day. Remote as the place was, the idea had seemed feasible.

'Of course Nadine loves the bright lights,' Aunt Mamie had said. 'All the same it's good to have a base, somewhere to come back to after her concert tours. And you, Andrea, have always loved the fells. I've the feeling they'll pull you back one day.'

However, with her usual good sense Aunt Mamie had been realistic when making her will. Left to her two nieces jointly the decision regarding the future of the house must be unanimous. They must both be present to discuss it in person with the executor, Martin Ackroyd of High Fell Farm, if they chose to sell.

Andrea turned swiftly to view again the desolation of the room. The contents of the upturned drawers were strewn heartbreakingly across the carpet. But what was this? Something she hadn't seen in years! She unscrewed the lid of the small, silver-topped jar and held it to her nose. The poignant potpourri fragrance wafted her back immediately to a perfect summer day and two little girls, herself and Nadine, playing on the lawn. She smelled the crushed grass and felt again her frustrated pain as Nadine danced about in triumphant glee at having got her own way once more in the game they were playing.

Was something born in that moment that changed her own feelings and gave her the determination to succeed later on in her chosen career? Startled, Andrea gazed down at the jar in her hand as if it could tell her that her recognition as a watercolour painter, not only, locally but farther afield, too, was partly due to years of Nadine's dominance.

It was a new thought, and she gazed at the jar of crushed rose petals in wonder. She had worked hard, desperately hard, but just lately she had begun to feel jaded. There was no necessity, now, to remain in London if she chose to make other plans. Silvergarth would provide a suitable place from which to work. For the first time since coming North Andrea's spirits lifted. A flash of sunlight pierced the grey that hung low over the hills. She unlatched the window and flung it wide open, revelling in the fresh, moorland air that caressed her face. So engrossed was she that the knocking on the front door only seeped into her, consciousness gradually. When at last she realised what it was she ran at once into the hall and clambered over the fallen curtains to pull the door open. The large man on the doorstep shot out his hand and took hers in a firm grip.

'Tom Gilmore,' he said. 'And you, no doubt, are Andrea?'

The flicker of surprised recognition in his eyes died away into a warm smile. She gasped, not recognising him for a moment in his light jacket and cream shirt.

'You!'

'You were expecting me?'

She stepped backwards over the curtains as he closed the door.

'Good grief!' he exclaimed, his penetrating glance sliding over the chaos in the hall.

'But who are you?' she asked. 'What are you doing here?'

'What's been going on? A break-in?'

He stared round in disbelief.

'The police . . .'

'It's taken care of,' Andrea said, rather stiffly. 'Why are you here? Was it something you wanted?'

He began to feel first in one jacket pocket and then in the other.

'It's here somewhere, the note I was given with my credentials so you'd let me in. I probably left it in the Land-Rover. No matter. I'll get it presently.'

He shot another look around the hall and then up at the wide staircase. Andrea began to feel in the way, as if it was she who had come blundering in. His sudden smile disturbed her in a way she found unnerving.

'I don't know what this is all about,' she said. 'I've had a tiring journey today, and I don't want to cope with anything more until tomorrow. Perhaps you could come back then.'

He moved towards the door and she thought he would leave. But he paused, looking back at her.

13

'My luggage is outside in the Land-Rover. I'll bring it in, and get that note for you at the same time.'

'Wait!' she cried. 'It's not a question of a note or your luggage. Please go now and come back tomorrow if you have to.'

His face warmed with a smile that lingered in his eyes.

'Have you been upstairs yet? You're not planning to stay here in this lonely place yourself, are you?'

For the first time she realised that if he chose not to go she had no means of making him. Her eyes went immediately to the wrenched-out telephone cable.

'It suits me if there's no-one else here,' he said. 'I'll have to give it a thorough examination in daylight tomorrow, of course. A lot would have to be cleared out, anyway, and alterations made to accommodate the numbers of youngsters I plan to have here.'

She stared at him in astonishment.

'What are you talking about?'

'It's the sort of place I'm after for my adventure base. Plenty of room for a games room and storage space for equipment and space for dumping things like filthy hiking gear. The lawn will make a fine football pitch.'

His eyes shone with enthusiasm.

'I need to get my head down for a bit. I didn't get any sleep last night.' He yawned. 'If you'll excuse me.'

14

'No!'

He drew his brows together and twisted his mouth.

'I was led to believe I'd be welcomed,' he said coldly.

'By whom?'

He looked surprised.

'Your sister, of course. Didn't she tell you?'

'Nadine!'

Andrea felt the blood leave her face and then shoot back.

'Where is she? Do you know where she is?'

'Back in London, I imagine. Where else?'

'Is she coming up to Silvergarth herself?'

He yawned as he started feeling in his pocket once more.

'Maybe, or maybe not. That's why I'm here on my own.'

'Surely she didn't tell you the house was for sale. If so, you're wasting your time.'

'It's not a question of purchase,' he said. 'Your sister . . .'

Andrea flung the door open.

'Please go.'

'If you say so.'

His gaze flicked upwards to the landing and then back at her.

'Go!' she said between clenched lips.

To her surprise, he did. She stood rigidly as he passed her, and then crashed shut the door. She heard the engine of a vehicle start up, and the crunch of tyres on the gravel. She moved to the staircase, and with one hand lightly on the banisters ran up the broad steps that wound round so elegantly to reach the landing. She went into each bedroom, steeling herself to look at the damage.

Poor, ravaged house! It needed looking after. There was no doubt at all now in her mind that she would come to live and work here herself.

CHAPTER TWO

There was a note from Sarah on the kitchen table next morning when Andrea came downstairs.

Martin phoned, it said in Sarah's thick handwriting. *He'll be in touch as soon as he can. I'm at the house.*

Andrea glanced at the clock on the mantelpiece. Ten o'clock! No wonder Sarah had gone already. Hastily she made coffee and drank it scalding hot. She almost ran along the track in her haste to get to the house and see what was happening.

No Land-Rover! That, at least, was something. Inside the open front door Sarah had removed the debris in the hall and folded the curtains in a pile on the chair. The hall looked much better, and felt so, too, with the purifying fresh air rushing in. Andrea found Sarah in the kitchen, her arms elbow-deep in the sink.

'There's been no sign of him,' she said as Andrea went in. 'That man who came, Tom Gilmore.'

To her surprise Andrea felt a tremor of disappointment. On her way over she had prepared herself mentally for a confrontation with him. Now she felt let down. However there was much to be done, and no time to think any more about it. Between them they cleared most of the disorder in the downstairs rooms, filling a bin with broken crockery and carrying it outside.

Andrea looked around, hesitating for a moment before following Sarah back inside. She told herself that her fingers were itching to get busy with her sketching pad on this lovely, bright morning, and that the chance of catching a glimpse of Tom Gilmore had nothing at all to do with it

'I'm off to the cottage now to see to lunch,' Sarah said at last.

Andrea nodded, intent on wiping the unit tops.

'I'll make a start upstairs now.'

The heavy, Victorian furniture upturned in her aunt's old room would have to wait until she had Sarah's help. She replaced the bedside table, and heaved the mattresses back on the bed. In the spare bedrooms along the landing the same mindless disorder was not quite so upsetting, and neither, to her surprise, was her own old room. There was little here in the room she had often used that mattered to her now. The curtains, damaged beyond repair, would have had to be replaced anyway, and most of the furniture had already been moved elsewhere.

Nadine's room, though, was a different matter. Appalled, Andrea stood on the threshold and stared. The familiar mustiness still hung about the room but the deep crimson curtains, were ripped to pieces lying on the carpet. Nadine had taken the utmost pains to see that her room remained unchanged during the periods she was away. Sarah had known better than to move the slightest thing if she hadn't wanted Nadine's wrath to fall on her.

Andrea picked up armfuls of the damaged curtains and placed them in a pile by the door. She heard a sound on the stairs. The door clicked open. Tom Gilmore stood on the threshold, unsmiling.

'Before you say anything, I've come to help.'

His voice was crisp and businesslike. Andrea gazed at him in silence.

With a swift glance he saw at once what had to be done. She marvelled at his strength as he righted the wardrobe and dressing-table and then moved to the other bedrooms to do the same. She wondered, too, at the momentous leap of her heart when he first appeared in the doorway.

When she had done all she could she came out on to the landing as he emerged from the end bedroom.

'Downstairs?'

He stood aside for her to go first. She was conscious of his hand on the banister rail behind her. At the bottom she hesitated, not looking at him, and then went towards the dining-room. She and Sarah had not been able to manage the heavy sideboard between them. Now he grabbed one end, motioning her to do the same at the other. She felt his power as he heaved at it and got it into position. She ran her hand over the polished wood and then looked up at him in silence. He had a slight cleft on his chin and the lines deepened in each cheek as he smiled.

'Thank you for your help,' she said as they went into the hall. 'I'm grateful.'

'I'd like to look round the house now, if I may, on my own.'

She thought instantly of what he had told her last evening about his crazy adventure-base scheme. She might have known there was some ulterior motive for his presence and the help he had given. Her loose hair danced round her face as she threw back her head

'No.'

He raised her eyebrows.

'It's as good a chance as any to reconnoitre on my own to see what's what. But if you object . . .'

'Object? I'd never agree to anything like that even if I didn't plan to live here myself. Surely I've made myself plain. You're wasting your time. The house is not on the market, and I certainly wouldn't agree to it being used for anything so bizarre.'

'But what's bizarre about an adventure base? It's a natural thing to consider in a house this size in such a good area.'

'The house is not on the market, to be sold or to be used for any other purpose.'

He picked, up a small paperweight and placed it in the centre of a polished side table. For a moment he gazed at it pensively. Then he looked up, an amused smile lightening his features.

'Not according to your sister.'

'Please, leave now.'

He seemed not to hear her words, but threw his head back and stared up at the wide staircase. Sunshine poured down through the window halfway up, highlighting the red lights in his fair hair.

'I mean it.'

Her voice cut into the silence like drops of ice.

For a long moment he stood there, unmoving, and she knew a stab of envy for her sister that he should take Nadine's word for something and not hers. Then he made a move towards the door.

'Have the police been in touch again? Any idea of who the culprits are, or what they were after?'

'Not yet.'

He stood aside in the doorway to let her go first, and waited on the top step while she made great play of locking the door. As she moved off across the lawn, Andrea resisted the temptation to glance back to check if he was watching her. She heard the engine of his Land-Rover with a jolt of relief. He seemed to take a long time to drive off, but at least he was on his way. She would think of him no more.

Overhead the sunlight trickled through the leaves of the horse chestnut tree, making swirling patterns on the grass. She walked towards the small gate that gave access to the track that was a short cut to Sarah's cottage. It was strangely difficult to put Tom Gilmore out of her mind. His calm assumption that he would get his own way made her smart, but she couldn't help a quickening of interest in the thought of his amused expression as he'd tried to con her into allowing an inspection of the house. There was about him, too, an air that gave her the feeling he was his own man with no intention of being influenced by anyone.

Andrea snapped shut the gate behind her. Were Nadine and this Tom Gilmore . . . She frowned, shaken again by an emotion she hadn't known for years. It was humiliating. She took a deep breath, determined to suppress it. She knew, with the suddenness of perfect truth, that she didn't want Tom Gilmore's name coupled with her sister's in any way.

The curtains at the open kitchen window swung gently in the breeze as Andrea went into the cottage. Sarah's plump face was

22

flushed and there was an air of excitement about her. She waved a hand at the tray on the sideboard.

'I've made you some sandwiches, lass. I've had mine. There've been a couple of phone calls.'

'Martin?'

'Aye. I said where you were. He'll call in later. Mary's been taken back into hospital. I could tell he's worried.'

'Oh, poor Mary. I'll try to get in to see her.'

'The other phone call will please you. A friend of yours. He saw my advert in the holiday guide, and he wants to book in next week.'

'Stephen!'

Andrea hoped she didn't sound as aghast as she felt. She swallowed, and smiled at Sarah who was beaming in approval.

'It's early in the year yet for visitors. The money'll be right useful. He'll have my bedroom. I'll be glad enough to sleep down here.'

Andrea gazed at her blankly.

'You can't do that, Sarah! Anyway, there's no need. I was going to tell you. I'm thinking of moving over to the house when we've finished clearing up over there. There's no problem.'

She would definitely move out if Stephen was coming. Hadn't she made it crystal clear that they could never be more than friends?

So why was he coming here?

Sarah picked up a duster.

'I've been upstairs sorting things out for him. He's been ill. He says the doctor ordered him out of London and he thinks the air here'll do him good.'

Andrea seated herself at one corner of the table with her plate of sandwiches in her hand.

'I didn't know that. I haven't seen Stephen for a week or two.'

She thought of Stephen's pale expression when she'd last seen him. He had always looked frail, but illness? He had made no attempt until`now to contact her. Maybe a rest was what he needed, but she wished he hadn't chosen to come here. It was as well she'd already made her decision about living and working in the house.

Unbidden, the tall figure of the man she had met for the first time yesterday came into her mind.

'Does this make sense to you, Sarah?' she asked. 'That man, Tom Gilmore, thinks he can run some sort of adventure base at Silvergarth. He said Nadine said he could.'

She broke off, confused.

'Nadine?'

Sarah's voice was hard. She stuffed her duster in her apron pocket and moved quickly towards the sink and stood with her back to Andrea.

'That'll never do.'

'I haven't told you properly yet, Sarah,' she said softly. 'I've made up my mind. I'm going to come back to Silvergarth permanently to work.'

'To live in the house like your aunt wanted?'

Andrea smiled.

'I want it, too. I'll go down to London every now and again for exhibitions, of course, but I'll be based up here.'

Sarah's eyes brightened as she smiled. Her obvious approval of the idea lightened Andrea's own spirits, and she smiled.

Andrea had plenty to occupy her thoughts as she drove down to Gardingley later in the afternoon. The small grey town, nestling in the surrounding hills, had a bustling air about it. As she walked up the main street she marvelled how her London life seemed to fall away from her, leaving the feeling that she had never been away at all. Perhaps Stephen's arrival would bring it back, but in the meantime she had things to do, the most important to purchase a supply of window locks for the house.

Back in the cottage with her purchases, she was pleased to hear that Sarah hadn't been idle either.

'I've been on the phone to a chap I know,' Sarah told her. 'He's a good worker. Said he'd do anything you want over at the house, lass.'

As she spoke there was the sound of a car

25

outside, and. Andrea flew to the window in time to see Martin Ackroyd emerge from his car and walk to the door. She opened it at once.

'Martin!' she cried in delight, running into his arms for a bear-like hug.

His hair was greying a little at the temples, and the lines round his eyes and mouth cut deeper than before. Martin was a dear friend, a rock, firm and dependable.

'How's Mary?' Andrea queried.

'Not so bad,' he replied.

She hated to see him so careworn and worried about his wife. No way was she willing to add to his burdens. She would sort out all her problems herself. He followed her inside where Sarah was already filling the kettle.

'Have you eaten?' she asked when she saw him.

'There'll be something waiting for me at the farm, Sarah. I just called in about the house. The police are no nearer solving the mystery of the break-in. They think people passing through the area were responsible. No doubt they're right. We'll have to be content with that for the time being.'

'The house won't be left empty any more,' Andrea said. 'I'm moving in as soon as we've cleared up.'

He frowned.

'It's a question about you being there on your own, Andrea. I don't like it after what's

26

happened.'

She waved her purchases at him.

'I've made a start on security. Window locks.'

Sarah shrugged.

'It's Andrea's own decision. Stubborn as they come.'

Andrea smiled at her.

'You need the room for your paying guest, Sarah. In any case I want to make Silvergarth my home now. The only thing is . . .'

Martin rubbed his hand over his lined forehead.

'Nadine's friend?'

Andrea looked at him in astonishment.

'You know about him? So Nadine's been in touch with you?'

He nodded.

'Late last night.'

'And?'

'You know Nadine. She wouldn't commit herself about when she's coming up, but she wants her friend to stay in the house until she gets here.'

'And you agreed?'

He looked troubled. Andrea opened her mouth to say more, but then thought better of it. Silvergarth was her sister's house, too. There was no reason why she shouldn't invite a guest to stay, but Tom Gilmore? The thin edge of the wedge if ever there was one. If she herself wasn't careful, the whole place would

27

seethe with people wrecking the calm atmosphere. But she mustn't worry Martin with any of this at the moment. She forced a smile.

'Don't worry about me, Martin. I'll be all right.'

He smiled back at her, obviously relieved.

Late next day, after hours of sorting and tidying at Silvergarth, Andrea found it impossible to endure any longer. The dust in her nostrils was insufferable. Running out swiftly to the back of the house she found relief in the cool air of the hillside behind as she started to climb.

Over the brow she sank down in the shelter on a lichen-covered boulder, and gazed at the expanse of bleak moorland in front of her. She leaned back and contemplated the view with pleasure. Feeling in the large pocket of her shirt for the pad and pencil she always carried she set to work in the hope of capturing something of the scene on paper. In the far distance some figures stirred. They were too far away to recognise who they were, but she had no doubt about who was leading them.

She stood up hurriedly, instantly reminded of Silvergarth House and the plans her sister and Tom Gilmore between them had made for it.

CHAPTER THREE

The window locks were soon in place in the house giving Andrea a sense of security. In the kitchen she unpacked the basket of provisions Sarah insisted she take with her. Then she tidied everything away. She would use her old bedroom for herself, and the large one at the back of the house as a make-shift studio. Facing north, the light was good there. The moorland views would provide inspiration if she needed any.

Enthusiasm bubbled up in her, and her fingers tingled for the feel of a paint brush in her hand. But first she must get her bed made up with the sheets and blankets Sarah had sent over.

'They'll be well-aired, lass,' Sarah had told her. 'Are you sure you won't be too lonely over there by yourself?'

No danger of that—far too many ideas floating around in her head, aching to be got down on paper.

Engrossed as she was, next day, in her sketch of the view from the back bedroom window, a vision of Tom Gilmore's tanned face kept invading her mind, making it hard to concentrate. At last she threw down her pencil. What was wrong with her that she could allow this to happen? Snapping her pad shut she went downstairs.

To her surprise, Sarah was in the kitchen, looking flushed, as if she'd hurried all the way from the cottage.

'Stephen wants to go out,' Sarah said. 'I said you'd go with him this first time, lass.'

'Stephen? Oh, yes, Stephen.'

Andrea sighed and then felt ashamed. She had almost forgotten him in her pleasure at moving into the house.

'He looks so lost, poor lad. I was thinking a trip out would do you both good. Somewhere like Howland Rocks maybe? It's a grand day.'

Andrea smiled as she removed her painting smock.

'I haven't sketched there for ages. How's Stephen settling in with you?'

Sarah's face lit up in a smile.

'Just grand. No trouble at all. He was up early inspecting the outside of the cottage. I asked him if he was going to paint it on paper or in real life.' Her stout frame shook with laughter.

'Anyroad, I gave him a good breakfast, and he looks all the better for it, but he needs to get some good strong air into his lungs. I thought I'd have a check around here, and see if anything wants doing. You'll drive round to the cottage to pick him up? I've packed lunch for you both.'

She looked so anxious for her to be gone that Andrea complied at once.

Stephen was ready and waiting, dressed in a pair of new jeans that made her own seem shabby. She saw him before he saw her, and was horrified at the change in him. He had always looked younger than his twenty-three years but now his face was thinner and there were dark circles beneath his eyes. He looked as if he needed a good long rest and some wholesome food. His eyes lit up as he saw her.

'Andrea! I swear you're even prettier. It's the air here, and the scenery. It's magnificent. All this open space! I'll be able to paint here.'

He didn't talk much as she drove down through Gardingley, but as they took the narrow road up to the beauty spot and he saw a few jagged pinnacles of rock he let out an exclamation of delight.

Parking the car, Andrea led the way up a narrow side path off the main track. Stephen craned his neck, staring in wonder at the rock formation that stood up from the hillside into the clear sky, like a giant stalagmite. He patted his pocket.

'I've got to sketch this.'

'Not yet, Stephen. Trust me. There's plenty more ahead.'

The intent look he gave her made her uneasy.

'I always trust you, love. You know that. Always.'

She thrust her loose hair behind her ears, and set off ahead of him up the winding, peaty

31

path through clumps of brown dusty heather. More magnificent rock formations towered above them. The heathery ground fell away steeply to their left, and the silver birch trees grew at incredible angles.

'If you don't mind, Stephen, I thought we'd sketch after lunch,' Andrea said. 'But first there's something for you to see.'

The path led out from the rocks. Ahead, beyond the stretch of grass, a grey stone house stood proudly on rising ground. They went up the steps and into the building. Andrea led the way through the people crowding the shop and up the stairs into a long, upper room that housed a collection of rocks and large posters and photographs. With a sigh of relief, Stephen sank down in one of the chairs in front of a screen set in the wall. Andrea looked at him anxiously.

'My pills,' he murmured, his face white. 'Right hand pocket'

She watched as he felt for them and slipped one beneath his tongue. To her relief the blue tinge round his lips began to fade.

'Those steps . . . took them too fast, that's all. I'll be all right.'

She could hardly believe it because he still looked so ill.

'Oh, Stephen!'

He smiled weakly.

'Don't worry, love.'

But how could she help it?

There was a clatter of feet on the bare floor. Andrea looked round in surprise at the rucksacks and stout boots on the boys and girls who came in uneasily and seated themselves on chairs, windowsill and floor. As their leader came forward to press the button to start the film Andrea gasped.

Tom Gilmore shot her a swift, appraising look that made the colour leap to her face. Self-consciously she moved farther apart from Stephen, astonished at seeing Tom there. She tried to concentrate on the film.

'Nothing much happened here for a million years,' the voice-over began.

For an instant Andrea's eyes met Tom's and a flicker of amusement flashed between them. Aware of the sudden turmoil of her heart she looked back at the screen. Why did he do this to her, and what did it mean? She didn't know, only that she was aware of his presence

Afterwards, in the crush of the shop downstairs, she turned to see where Stephen was and saw him at the counter examining postcards. Tom, nearby, was chatting to a group who clustered round him. How young Stephen looked compared to him. Tom's magnetism seemed to drain all Stephen's personality. She felt it as she stood waiting, acutely conscious of Tom's large figure.

'Do you know him?' Stephen asked as they went outside. 'He seemed to know you. He

33

was staring at you a lot.'

Andrea shrugged, trying to look unconcerned.

'He's a friend of my sister, that's all. This way, Stephen. I thought we'd picnic now, and get some coffee at the kiosk later.'

He seemed content to follow her to the other side of the hillside to where the ground sloped away from a grassy clearing. Beyond were rough, stonewall-encased fields and hills stretching mistily into the distance.

'Perfect,' he said in satisfaction. 'It's incredible. Thanks, Andrea.'

'For what?'

'For everything. For being here, with me. We'll come again, won't we, and bring our painting gear?'

Andrea smiled as she handed Stephen one of the huge, salad-filled sandwiches Sarah had prepared.

'You'll come with me?'

He didn't wait for her answer, but got up and wandered off, still eating, to examine the odd, oval shape of the rock behind them. Then he was back again, smiling and relaxed, seeming content to eat the rest of their meal in silence. But as Andrea began to pack the containers back into her bag he put his hand on hers and looked at her beseechingly.

'Three years difference in age isn't much. I know I'm younger than you, love, but . . .'

He looked so boyish that she let her hand

lie beneath his.

'We've talked about this before,' she said gently. 'Nothing's changed.'

'But it could, if you give me the chance.'

She looked at him compassionately, blaming herself for perhaps giving him hope when there was none. A friendly interest in his work had started it though she had made her feelings clear almost at once. She shivered, and smoothed her hair back behind her ears.

'Shall we get a coffee back at the kiosk?'

Her words seemed to hang in the air. Then he smiled and pulled a piece of charcoal and a pad from his jacket pocket.

'I'll catch up with you in a minute.'

She picked up the bag taking him at his word and glad to be on her own for a short time. Her path took her past more sheer formations, and she was surprised to hear the sound of voices as she approached. Then she saw roped figures climbing up the rockface ahead of her. She seated herself on a boulder to watch them for a few moments.

They were obviously having lessons because a series of instructions were bawled continuously down at them from above. She could see now that each climber made the ascent on his own but was roped securely to someone at the bottom and presumably also at the top. Raising her eyes, the tall figure of Tom Gilmore was silhouetted against the sky.

He stood there with his fair head bent

forward: He hadn't seen her, of course, because his attention was fixed on the climber negotiating the sheer face below him. She could easily have moved away, but something held her there. She watched, enthralled, as the figure slowly manoeuvred its way to the top. Tom, his broad shoulders held back now, let out a shout of triumph.

The next climber, though, seemed frightened as the climb began. Tom leaned over so far she thought he would fall, and his booming shout of encouragement echoed among the rocks. Andrea had never felt the slightest desire to do anything so foolhardy, and yet, sitting watching them, she could see the excitement in it, the exhilaration and sense of achievement experienced in conquering something difficult. There was the sharing of responsibility, too. She had always liked to be on her own, a solitary spirit making her own decisions. Now she began to see a value in knowing that the team members depended on each other for their well-being.

Stephen's voice beside her made her jump.

'How I envy them.'

She made room for him beside her on the rock. His pale eyes shone with enthusiasm

'It's the team spirit. I like that. We could have it, too, in a small way, you and me, Andrea.'

She sat still, her eyes on the climber now

nearing the top, resisting the temptation to move away from Stephen. He looked at her strangely for a moment, and then half closed his eyes.

'I want to give you everything I've got,' he said in a low voice.

He took hold of her hand and she allowed it to lie passively in his. Suddenly, loud shouts of triumph filled the air. The climber had made it. At the top the others crowded round. Tom Gilmore was grinning and looked around him. Suddenly Andrea felt his gaze fixed on her.

Oh, horrors, she was blushing! Her free hand flew to her face, but she was unable to look away. There was something in his intent gaze that held hers. She wondered if Stephen was aware of it. For a moment Tom stood quite still. Then there was a scramble around him of packing up. One by one the figures vanished, presumably to negotiate an easier way down on the other side. Andrea let out a long breath.

'Don't,' Stephen said, releasing her hand and standing up. 'I've made a fool of myself again, haven't I?'

At the kiosk, they bought coffee and as they stood drinking it the boys and girls appeared. They looked dirtier now, but there was a cheerful bustle about them as they ordered a variety of things to eat and drink. Stephen drained his cup quickly, and waved his hand towards the looming rocks.

'Have another coffee, Andrea, while I do a quick sketch over there.'

She watched him move off.

'Move back, you lot,' a voice called. 'The lady wants more coffee.'

She turned to see Tom Gilmore's sardonic eyes on her. Flushing slightly, she moved towards the counter and then found him beside her, ordering coffee for himself and paying for hers. A warmth seemed to shine from him. She moved back slightly to escape the effect it seemed to be having on her. For goodness' sake, she had only known him a brief time and most of that had been spent fighting his incredible intention of taking over her home.

'So, you've lost your companion.'

He gave such a heavy emphasis to the last word she felt colour creep into her cheeks. She turned away so that he shouldn't see. There was no way she was going to explain Stephen to him. Let him think what he liked.

They moved aside from the crowd around the kiosk, and stood on a slight rise, close together. He took a gulp of coffee and then smiled at her, the lines deepening at the sides of his mouth.

'Any news of your sister?'

So he hadn't any news either. She looked up at him suspiciously, wondering what he was planning behind that smile of his.

38

'Nadine will be in touch in her own good time.'

He nodded.

'This is the last day for this group. That's why we're here. It's the climax for them, rock climbing. They've done a grand job. See much of it?'

'A bit, It looked highly dangerous.'

His eyes laughed at her.

'Not when you know how.'

She shuddered.

'Those steep slopes!'

'We'll make a rock climber of you yet, you'll see.'

His eyes narrowed as he looked over at the group of boys and girls.

'My young partners are here somewhere. You'd better meet them before we move into the house.'

She drew in a quick breath.

'Aren't you taking a lot on yourself?'

'It won't be long before we're all together at Silvergarth. You'll have to get used to it.'

He downed his coffee.

'You can see what a fine job we'll do for these young people. You mustn't let your envy of your sister stand in her way as in the past. It won't do, you know, not anymore.'

Andrea stared at him, speechless. Her hand shook, and some coffee splashed on her jacket. She wiped it off hurriedly. What on earth had Nadine told him about her? A pack of lies by the sound of it. But there was no time to ask because Stephen was back, and the boys and girls were shouting to Tom to hurry up. It took all her willpower not to stamp furiously after them all to have it out with him on the spot.

Earlier, watching Tom's encouraging concern, she had felt a stirring for his aims and plans. But now he had put an iron barrier between them with mention of Nadine and his certainty that she, herself, was in the wrong. She knew her sister only too well. It was plain that Nadine wanted Tom, and would have him by whatever means. What else had she told him that wasn't true? His easy belief of them was surprisingly hurtful.

Andrea gave a little shrug, feeling a surge of frustration as she unlocked her car door. Very soon now, Tom Gilmore would be moving into Silvergarth unless she came up with a very good way to stop him.

40

CHAPTER FOUR

Andrea was pleased with her output of sketching in the days that followed even though she had not yet worked out a solution to her problem. She wished she had asked Martin Ackroyd how she could contact Tom Gilmore. It was too much to expect she would find him still wandering around in the area before he moved in.

But that was exactly what happened! She was walking from the house along the track to Sarah's cottage when she saw him consulting a map, finding difficulty in holding it open in the blustery wind. At her approach he smiled at her with such warmth she was suspicious, remembering with a flush of anger the insinuations he'd made about her the last time they met.

'I'm on my way to the gorge,' he said, folding the map. 'Shall we walk together since we're going the same way? I understand it's a suitable place for abseiling.'

She hardly heard what he said as she concentrated on keeping up with his long strides.

'You owe me an explanation,' she said rather breathlessly.

He stopped and swung round to face her.

'An explanation? Then walk farther with

me and tell me about it.'

'Nadine gave you the wrong idea about me. She wants you to think . . .'

He gave a short laugh.

'I make up my own mind. No-one tells me what to think.'

There seemed no answer to that, and she was silent as they entered the gorge and began to walk along the path by the river. She shivered a little at the gloom from the overhanging trees though there was welcome shelter from the wind. He paused, looking upwards with that appraising look she was beginning to know well.

'Fine,' he said in satisfaction. 'Those steep cliffs that are bare of trees will be useful for a first lesson in abseiling. Yes, we'll do well here. We've got a camp going down in Gardingley at the moment. It's not ideal, of course, being so far away. That's why we need Silvergarth for a permanent base. We can take more people then. Nadine's in full agreement.'

He looked at her speculatively.

'What's wrong with you, making all this fuss about your sister's life? You couldn't get away from the place fast enough three years ago, I believe.'

She glared back at him, unable to deny it. She had left Silvergarth, needing to be near London and the galleries where she had planned to exhibit her work. She had worked

42

hard, but now her presence there was not as necessary as at first when she was trying to get established.

'So what's wrong?' he said. 'Nadine's ambitious, and so are you. From what she said, it seems you share the same ambitious drive, the same need to surge ahead come what may.'

'But not to trample others under foot.'

He laughed.

'And you think Nadine does that?'

She looked at him in silence. Impossible, now it came to the point, to insist on knowing exactly what else Nadine had said about her without implying even more criticism of her sister. Impossible, too, to tell him she couldn't reconcile his own bursting energy and love of danger with Nadine's dislike of outdoor life. Her sister had always been an indoor person and had shuddered when Andrea had gone off in all weathers to sketch on the surrounding fells.

She saw the muscles ripple in his throat as he threw his head back to look upwards to where the line of bending trees at the top of the gorge met the pale sky.

'Imagine it,' he said, his voice ringing with confidence. 'The freedom to be themselves for all those boys and girls. Some of them have never had a chance. That's what I want to do, give them a chance.'

His eyes alight with enthusiasm, he started

43

to expound some of his theories to her, and in spite of herself she found her interest come alive.

'Remember the film commentary at the Rocks?' he said quirking one eyebrow at her. 'Nothing much happened for a million years?'

He gave a roar of laughter that rang between the narrow cliffs.

'That's what I call stability! It's what those youngsters need, stability, and in the right place I can give it to them. It's not nearly enough to have them camping in the area for only a few days. Two, three or four weeks and we can give them something really worthwhile.'

They walked for a few moments in silence. Then, pausing to hold back a branch of an overhanging ash, he said, 'I'm lucky in my partners. Anna's on the same wavelength as them, and there's nothing Terry won't tackle. But we need a base like Silvergarth.'

Now was the moment to ask him how her sister had become involved, but Andrea's tongue seemed stuck in her mouth. There was something utterly compelling in Tom's conviction of the rightness of his plans. It seemed to her, quite suddenly, that here was a man to be reckoned with. Perhaps that was his attraction for Nadine. Those blue eyes of his held some magic quality that made others do his bidding. He was dangerous!

'So when are you expecting Nadine?' she

asked to hide her confusion.

'Today, tomorrow, who knows? Soon, anyway. Meanwhile I shall get my things to the house. The path goes high above the river here. Seen enough, have you? I shall have to get back.'

It was crazy, she thought, as they retraced their steps. She accompanied him with every intention of finding out in detail his plans regarding the house, but was no wiser than when talking to Martin. For all that Tom Gilmore's expectations were so reasonable there might well be a hidden catch if Nadine was involved.

'The house is half mine,' she said.

He grinned at her.

'So I understand. I promise not to get in your way. Somewhere to sleep is all I need at the moment, that's all. And somewhere to store some of our expensive caving equipment where it can be kept dry and safe.'

They reached the cottage. He stood looking at it, without speaking for a long, appraising moment.

'There's more than one room downstairs?' he said. 'How many bedrooms?'

Andrea stiffened. He could keep his hands off Sarah's cottage. She murmured something, and to her relief he didn't pursue the subject. Just then, the door opened and Stephen came out. His face lit up with a smile.

'Andrea! Come and have a cuppa with me.

Sarah's got the kettle on.'

She smiled and waved. Tom gave her a curt nod before walking off swiftly towards the house.

She didn't see Tom Gilmore again until much later, back at Silvergarth. There, was the sound of crashing in the room that he had taken for himself along the landing from her own. Emerging from her room, she was surprised to see him in a royal blue towelling robe with a white towel slung round his shoulders. He quirked an eyebrow at her.

'The bathroom?'

She pulled her own robe tightly round her, annoyed to feel herself flush. 'After you,' she said coldly.

With a broad smile he took her at her word and she retreated to her room.

At least he could have insisted she go first! She sat on the edge of her bed, and when at last he tapped on her door to indicate the bathroom was free she made no answer and waited a long while before emerging on to the landing again.

*　　　*　　　*

Andrea had been anticipating her sister's arrival but when Nadine stepped out of a taxi the next afternoon she was taken completely by surprise. With her, naturally, was Tom Gilmore.

46

They arrived as Andrea was returning from a day's sketching, having promised herself a quick shower before going over to Sarah's for a meal. She saw the car, and stood transfixed. Nadine, in striking scarlet and black, gazed round her with interest while Tom paid the fare and then picked up two of the massive suitcases. He hadn't seen Andrea, but her sister had. Nadine stared at her in silence before permitting herself a brief smile. Andrea followed them into the hall.

'I wasn't sure when to expect you, Nadine,' she said hesitantly.

Tom turned immediately at her voice, smiling with a warmth that contrasted with Nadine's chilly greeting.

'So there you are, Andrea. I thought you'd vanished into the morning mist,' he said with a friendly smile.

'I have work to do,' she said.

She didn't add that this morning she had made herself scarce deliberately, not wanting to be in the house while he was settling himself into her home.

As her sister was concerned for the moment in organising the carrying of her luggage to her room Andrea made her escape up the wide staircase. As she towelled herself dry after her shower she wondered about Nadine's immediate plans. There was some food in the house, Sarah had seen to that, but her own main meals were to be taken at the

47

cottage.

'It's only good sense,' Sarah had said. 'I'm cooking for the two of us, Stephen and me, so one more'll not make much difference. It won't take long for you to come over here and it leaves you free to paint, which is what you want, Andrea.'

True, of course, and she was grateful, but no way would Sarah invite Tom and her sister. They would need to make their own arrangements she thought as she fastened a silver brooch at the neck of her pink silk blouse.

It seemed, when she went downstairs, that Tom had arrangements well in hand.

'I've booked a table at the Gardingley Arms,' he told her as they stood in the hall. 'You'll join us, Andrea?'

This was so unexpected that Andrea felt a flush of colour in her cheeks.

'Thank you, no. Sarah's invited me to the cottage,' she replied.

His smile faded.

'Yes, I should have realised.'

He was silent for a moment, and then said, 'Your sister wishes to speak with you. She'll be down soon. We won't be leaving for another half hour.'

Andrea nodded, smoothing her hair behind her ears. She was in no immediate hurry. She moved towards the shifting-room door, and as she did so heard a call from the staircase.

48

Turning, she gave a gasp of surprise. Nadine, with the light from the window behind her, looked like a Greek goddess in a pure white swirling dress. Her fair hair, piled on top of her head, sparkled with diamante stones at her brow, and in her ears hung long diamond earrings.

Beside her Andrea felt Tom start, and smiled herself at the impression she knew her sister would create at the modest Gardingley Arms. It seemed to her that Tom let out a short laugh, too. For a second there was a mocking light in his blue eyes or had she merely imagined it? The expression on his face was serious now as he gazed at Nadine. As she reached them, Nadine eyed Andrea's simple attire with obvious amusement.

'You're not dining with us then, Andrea?' she asked pointedly.

'I have other plans,' Andrea said rather stiffly.

'With the boyfriend?' Tom cut in.

She ignored him.

'First, though, I'd like an opportunity to talk, Nadine. We haven't seen each other for so long.'

She indicated the door to the sitting-room. To her relief Tom had the tact not to follow them. As Andrea closed the door, Nadine moved towards the window and stood pensively for a moment. Then, seeming to come suddenly to life, she moved to the grand

49

piano, opened the lid and ran her hands over the keys in an ugly staccato beat. It seemed to Andrea like the fragmentation of her own hopes for the future of the house.

It was a warm evening, but suddenly the room seemed cold. Fluffy clouds floated across the evening sky. Then Nadine stopped playing.

'This instrument's badly out of tune. I'll arrange for it to be attended to.'

Arranging herself in one of the deep armchairs, she looked expectantly at her sister. Andrea sat down, too, hardly knowing how to begin. She and Nadine had drifted so far apart as to be almost strangers.

'The house,' she said abruptly. 'I don't really know what your future plans are, Nadine, but even to consider turning it into an adventure base, you can't do it. I want to live here myself.'

'So?'

Nadine arched her perfect eyebrows. She looked faintly amused.

'It's my house, too, you know. I've a perfect right to invite whom I choose to stay here.'

Andrea bit her lip. Silvergarth had always been a place her sister hated. It was hard to envisage Nadine here helping to turn it into a holiday base. In fact she knew it couldn't possibly work out. It seemed more like a ruse than ever to get her, Andrea, to agree to part with her share of the property.

50

She looked at Nadine through narrowed eyes. Nadine shrugged.

'This great mausoleum of a place, could you afford to buy me out, Andrea, and would you really want to?'

The triumphant gleam in Nadine's eyes was too much. Andrea sprang up. Nadine smiled languidly and went on.

'I'm being practical, that's all. I shall invite Tom to remain, and there's nothing you can do about it, or about, having his crowd of youngsters here indefinitely at my invitation.'

'Suppose I find I'm in a position to buy your share of the house and you both move elsewhere?'

Nadine looked knowing as she rose to her feet. How maddening she was! They both knew it wasn't possible. The interview appeared to be at an end without much having been said. Andrea made another attempt as they went out into the hall.

'Nadine, what are you going to do now? Your concerts . . . are you . . .'

Her sister turned with her hand on the banister.

'Don't make a silly fuss about Tom being here. He'll cope.'

There was the sound of a door opening and Tom came running swiftly down the stairs towards them. He looked almost a stranger in his dark suit. His crisp white shirt emphasised his tanned features. He smiled, and its warmth was directed at Nadine. Andrea was used to being overlooked in her sister's presence, but now she felt a strange hurt.

'All sorted out?' he said. 'Then we'll go.'

His easy assumption that she would agree with everything her sister said made Andrea gasp, and she was still seething when she arrived at Sarah's cottage.

After their meal, Sarah encouraged Andrea and Stephen to go out and enjoy the mild evening.

'I'm going to have a good clear-up,' she said. 'Get off, the pair of you. It'll do you good.'

Andrea smiled at Sarah's preoccupied air as she started to clear the table. They were obviously not needed here.

'I'll just get my jacket,' she said. 'We'll have to go over to the house for the car.'

They walked by the river down in Gardingley, Andrea still rather silent. Here the water was smooth-flowing. So soothing were the effects of the hills rising steeply on the other side and the shady trees on the river bank that she began to feel the tension slip away from her.

'You can see every single stone on the walls up there on the hill,' Stephen said. 'The air's incredibly clear.'

He felt in his pocket and produced paper and a short stick of charcoal He was instantly absorbed. Andrea seated herself on a fallen tree trunk to wait while he made his sketch. On the other side of the river the late sun glinted on the windows of a low stone house. It looked peaceful against the background of hills. She saw that Stephen was making it the focal point of his sketch.

'Isn't that beautiful?' he called to her. 'I wouldn't mind living there one day, with you. What a situation!'

He was silent after that and she knew his thoughts were mere fantasy and that he knew it in his secret heart. He looked so pale, she thought. If only he had half Tom Gilmore's vigour! Leaning back a little she closed her eyes, and immediately a vision of Tom's smiling face sprang into her mind. She recalled Tom in evening clothes that made him look taller, more refined. There was an instant's warmth round her heart before she remembered Nadine, too, in her beautiful white gown descending the staircase towards him. At once Andrea sat up straight, eyes wide open, pained beyond understanding at the thought of Tom Gilmore and her sister together.

CHAPTER FIVE

Sunshine and shadow intermingled in a scene so full of atmosphere as Andrea climbed the fells a few days later that she was enchanted. She had set out with her painting gear in a mood of lightness that hadn't been with her for a long time.

There was a sense of freedom in it that she welcomed. Each day since Nadine's arrival she had made sure she was out of the house before she heard any sounds of stirring from the other two. Where they went each day or what they did she had no idea. Presumably most of their meals were eaten out because the kitchen was left undisturbed.

She found, though, that the empty kitchen accentuated her own loneliness because she knew that Tom and Nadine were together at least some of the time. Her only escape from it was to work, and work hard. Today she wanted to catch some of the cloud formations above High Top with the ancient farmhouse nestling below. Settling herself in a small clearing among heather, she set to work.

The hours passed swiftly, and she was surprised to find that it was midday when she glanced at her watch. She put down her brush, and stretched her arms above her head, suddenly aware that she was hungry. When she was working she lost all sense of time. Now it felt as if she was dragged back hastily into the world and reality. She rummaged in her bag for her packet of bread and cheese, and was just pouring coffee from her flask when she saw signs of life in the distance. No doubt it was the group of boys and girls she had seen the other day at the Rocks with Tom.

She looked for Tom in vain as they came close, expecting them to pass by on the track. Instead one or two broke away from the group and came running towards her.

'Come back, you lot!' a voice boomed.

'It's OK, Anna,' one of them shouted back. 'Just a quick look and we'll catch you up.'

They stood behind Andrea, gazing at the painting.

'It's great,' one of the girls said. 'Did you do that?'

She came to the side and gazed at Andrea with luminous grey eyes. Her rather thin hair was scraped back off her face and tied back with an elastic band. She looked almost too frail to be up here in the wilds clad in hiking gear. Her companions laughed, slapping her on the back.

'Who else, stupid?'

Andrea smiled as she raised her cup to her lips.

'Do you like it?'

'It's great.'

There were more shouts, and most of them were off at once towards the rest of the group. Only the girl remained.

'Is it hard to do?' she asked. 'Could I do it?'

Andrea looked at her speculatively.

'You just have to try, that's all. It's like lots of things. Unless you try you'll never know if you can do it. But if you really want to and work hard at learning the techniques there's no reason why you shouldn't find you're as good as anyone else.'

'Come on, Susie!' another bellow came.

At once Susie was off, too. Andrea watched her join the rest of the group with a little ache in her heart. Where was Tom today? If only he had come striding through the heather, the glow of vitality on his tanned face and in his eyes a warm smile for her! Holding her coffee cup poised, she imagined how it would feel. There was a warmth about him that brought joy to her heart in spite of knowing that all his thoughts were for her sister. But there was no harm in dreaming, was there?

After that it was hard to concentrate. She began to pack away her things. This was the last day of Stephen's holiday. It would be only kind to call at the cottage to offer him a lift to the station for the following morning since she could do no more good here.

She found Stephen in the garden, gazing at the front of the cottage. He turned at Andrea's approach and his face lit up with pleasure. She smiled.

'I thought I'd come over to see if there was anything I could do.'

'Come and sit down and talk for a minute, Andrea.'

He bent to pick up something rustling in the grass and she saw, to her delight, that it was a kitten. He held it out.

'Meet Silver. Sarah found him in the lane. Don't know how he got there.'

Andrea stroked the soft grey fur.

'He's lovely!'

Stephen cradled the little thing against him as she seated herself beside him on the warm stone wall.

'He's for you, Andrea.'

'For me?'

His eyes shone at her.

'Sarah isn't keen on cats. She was all for leaving him there, but I couldn't do that. You'll look after him, love him, won't you?'

How could she refuse? She took the kitten and laid him in her lap. His purr shook his young body.

'The only thing is I'll have to go down to London soon and get some of the pieces I've done to the Gallery and see what Rupert thinks. But perhaps I can find someone to look after Silver for me.'

There was a hopeful light in Stephen's eyes.

'You'll be coming to London? So I'll see you?'

'You know the score, Stephen. There's been no pretence, ever, and that's the way it has to be. You know that. In any case, I'll only be down there a couple of nights.'

To her own ears her voice sounded cold, but there was no help for it. She knew how it would be if she didn't make a final stand now. He looked at her in silence for a moment, his face paler, than ever. Then, to her relief, he seemed to accept what she said, but the smile he gave her wrung her heart.

She hated partings, and this one was sadder than most because she knew she wouldn't be seeing much, if anything, of Stephen in the weeks ahead. Suddenly she had a strong feeling that they would never meet again. She tried to shrug it off, but the feeling persisted as she carried young Silver home to Silvergarth.

In the days that followed, Andrea tried to immerse herself in her work, but continually found herself pausing and gazing into space for no reason at all. She had done her best to avoid Tom, and had succeeded to the extent of hardly knowing he was in the house. Nadine, though, was another matter since her belongings were scattered everywhere except in the kitchen.

'This won't do,' Andrea told the kitten sternly. 'I've got to decide what I'm going to do with you when I go down to London.'

She picked him up and rubbed his soft grey

fur against her face. Opening the back door she carried him out into the garden and placed him on the grass. Immediately he rubbed himself round her ankles, purring loudly.

'We need some more cat food,' she told him. 'A trip down to Gardingley to stock up, I think. We don't want you to starve, do we?'

Silver scuttled off into the rose bushes. Smiling, Andrea collected her car keys and shopping bag.

Later, as she emerged from the post office in the little town, she saw Tom walking towards her. She stopped in confusion. A burst of sunlight cast shadows on his cheeks. His sweatshirt was the same shade of deep blue as his eyes. He stopped as they met.

'I'm glad I've seen you, Andrea. There's something I need to say.'

She moved her shopping bag from one hand to the other, and he moved forward to take it.

'Allow me.'

But she held on to it, staring at him as if he was some sort of stranger. So much had changed since last she'd seen him. Stephen was back in London for one thing. Tom gave a slight shrug.

'Let's get some coffee.'

Hardly realising how it came about Andrea found herself seated opposite Tom in the window of the small café next door to the post office. He ordered coffee and a plate of cream cakes. She looked at them in dismay.

'What are you trying to do, fatten me up?'

His smile produced half moons of lines in his cheeks that, strangely, made him feel younger.

'You look as if you could do with it. Your skin is almost transparent.'

Startled at his personal criticism of her, she almost spilled her coffee. She placed the cup carefully back in the saucer.

'I'm sorry,' he said. 'I feel concerned about you, Andrea, that's all. I feel I've added to the problem about the house and come between you and your sister in a way that wasn't intentional.'

He picked up the plate of cakes and held it towards her. She took one and he did, too.

'I'm planning on going down to London to collect my gear,' she said.

She thought of the gallery and her studio flat. Maybe seeing them again would help her see what her future life should be.

He picked up his cup.

'Nadine's off for a couple of nights, too.'

She thought suddenly of the kitten.

'Could you . . . if you're at the house . . .'

He raised his eyebrows and she felt herself flush, hating to ask a favour of him but knowing she must.

'I'll need someone to feed my kitten while I'm away. He's no trouble. Could you?'

He laughed and the sound was loud in the small room.

'Why not? He's a nice little thing. I've seen him about the place.'

Draining his cup, he beckoned the waitress to bring more coffee.

'I had a kitten once, as a young lad; just before my parents died. I was allowed to keep him for a short time until they decided what to do with me.'

She looked at him in surprise.

'Do with you?'

'My parents died in a car accident when I was ten.'

'Oh, and were you hurt, too?'

'Only slightly. I was lucky to emerge from the car almost unscathed. I lived with an uncle in Surrey for a while, until I went to my prep school in Dorset. Then I went to public school.'

'And the kitten?' she asked quickly.

'Given away, I'm afraid.'

She felt a surge of compassion. He had told her only the bare details but she could sense the pain behind it all.

'I'm sorry,' she murmured.

As he sipped his coffee, she looked at him thoughtfully, remembering the care he had shown his boys and girls on their rock-climbing activities. No wonder he prized stability so highly after his early experiences.

'So the kitten's settling down at

Silvergarth?' he said.

A deep feeling of peace began to flow through her in spite of the noise and chatter around them. As he smiled at her she felt warm, content.

'Is there any likelihood of the cottage down the track coming on the market?' he said. 'I've heard the odd rumour.'

Andrea gazed at him in surprise.

'Not as far as I know.'

He sat up straight, his sudden forcefulness immediately swamping her own feelings of sympathy. She hadn't liked his interest in the cottage last time they met. Suddenly she felt on her guard against him again, and she didn't like it. Taking a sip of her coffee, she felt the sharpness of the look he gave her. Then he seemed to relax again as he tilted his head back to drain his cup.

'The cottage has a lot of potential. It could be a real asset to me. There's land behind, isn't there? If planning permission's obtained to expand the old building we could really make something of it.'

Andrea's laugh was louder than she intended.

'We? Aren't you and Nadine taking a lot on yourselves?'

She could see he was deadly serious. He leaned across the table.

'Haven't you ever been single-minded when something meant a great deal to you?'

62

'Ruthless, you mean?'

He grinned.

'It gets things done, I find, and something needs to be done. Our adventure holidays are based on three principles—self-reliance, positive thinking and the concept of leaving people and places better than you found them. To do more good we have to expand. With our combined resources, Nadine's and mine, it's possible to put Silvergarth in order and make any necessary alterations. Even better would be to use the cottage in the scheme at the same time.'

Andrea hesitated, biting her lip.

Even if your adventure base plan means a lot to you, she wanted to say, it means nothing to Nadine so where will that leave you when she goes on to someone new?

But she couldn't say it. Instead she asked what it was he had wanted to say to her. For a moment he looked thoughtful. Then he smiled.

'The cottage,' he said simply. 'We need it. Will you use your influence with Sarah to obtain it for us, persuade her to sell?'

Andrea gasped.

'Do you really think I'd have anything to do with that?'

She rose, and pushed her chair as far as it would go beneath the table.

'Thanks for the coffee,' she said, a little breathlessly. 'I must go now.'

And she did just that, vanishing before he had time to pay the bill and follow her and continue his pressure. What Tom had said about wanting the cottage was disturbing. She would go to London for her things tomorrow and put it right out of her mind.

*　　*　　*

Emerging from the taxi at the Rainbow Gallery, Andrea felt a great feeling of release as she breathed in the noisy London air. The owner of the gallery, Rupert Burton, was delighted to see her. As she walked through the swing doors into the hushed, carpeted vestibule with her arms full he came forward with both arms outstretched and caught her in a quick embrace.

'My darling, Andrea.'

He looked as broad as ever, his bald head as shiny and his black suit as immaculate as if it had just been delivered from his tailor. His bow tie was a deep shade of magenta. It was good to see him.

'Back with us at last. For keeps, I trust.'

His eyes darted to the folders she had brought with her.

'You have something to show me?'

This was her old, familiar life, and Andrea smiled as she placed her work on the polished table. Swiftly he examined each watercolour painting.

'Ah,' he breathed. 'Divine! The same delicacy, the same perfection of detail.'

With a painful stab, a vision of the fells above Silvergarth shot into Andrea's mind. She saw Tom in heavy boots and bulky hiking gear.

Rupert gave a sigh of pleasure as he replaced her work in the folders.

'But you're looking thinner, my sweet.'

She gave a shaky laugh before commenting, 'Someone else said that.'

'May I have the pleasure of taking, you to lunch?'

'You may, Rupert, thanks. But am I allowed to view your exhibition first?'

'Of course, your excellency. Follow me, if you please.'

The tension of the last weeks began to slip from her as they went up the grey-carpeted staircase. Massive, shiny-leafed plants stood in every niche.

'You've changed the decor,' she said.

It sounded like criticism, but she didn't mean it that way. Rupert loved change as she well knew. But she understood the muted colour scheme when she saw the large, colourful oil paintings in huge frames. The contrast was electric, and she exclaimed in delight.

Later, in the restaurant, soft music provided a soothing background, and the rich red carpet and walls created friendliness and warmth. Rupert ordered for her, as she leaned back in her chair with a feeling of deep pleasure. He was an entertaining companion. Afterwards they lingered over coffee and liqueurs.

'It's been a wonderful day,' she said as he lit a cigar.

'Must you return to that deserted place?'

Immediately she was transformed to the small Gardingley café with Tom leaning towards her with the light of fanaticism in his eyes. The pain of it was almost physical. She wanted to cry out that she knew no other life in which she felt so totally alive, the call of the northern fells was in her blood. She could consider no other life now, however painful being near Tom Gilmore would be.

Back at her small flat she set about packing up her belongings. It was past midnight before she finished. The place looked bare now, of course, and totally unlike the comfortable place she had made it during her three-year occupancy. So it was with relief that she drove North next day. She seemed to have been away from Silvergarth for years.

When at last she drew up in the drive in the late afternoon, it surprised her to discover that Nadine had not yet returned. Tom's Land-Rover wasn't there either. She had expected to see it in its usual place. Now she felt unaccountably empty inside when she should have been relieved at not having to withstand another bombardment about the cottage.

She had eaten on the way up and didn't need anything else for the moment. She would unpack the car, and check that the kitten was all right. Then she would take a shower and go out to sketch for a while. Silver emerged from under the table as she went into the kitchen, a purring grey ball. It was good to see him so happy and well-cared for. Tom had done his job well.

She hesitated, reluctant after all to go out and leave Silver behind. Tom had fed him, stroked him, and she felt near to Tom because of it. But this was ridiculous! She smiled ruefully at herself as she made her preparations.

CHAPTER SIX

The glorious day was declining into evening as she chose a spot where the hillside dipped to accommodate a beck beneath silver birch trees. Satisfied, she settled herself on a mossy rock. The delicate detail of slanting sunlight on the brown rippling water was pleasing.

She was unaware of passing time as she worked. She saw only the shadows in the indents in the boulders on the other bank, and felt the strength in their very silence and immobility. There was an agelessness here that was appealing. Until now there had seemed to be a sense of stability lacking in her own life. Now, having brought the remainder of her belongings to Silvergarth, she would surely find it again.

Absorbed, she mixed delicate shades of yellowy-green on her palette, and didn't at first hear the footsteps coming along the path. She looked up for a moment; and then down again, conscious of the warmth from Tom's body as he stood behind her and gazed silently at her work.

'Too restricted,' he said at last as he moved round and seated himself on a rock facing her.

His hair caught the last of the sunlight and the brown skin on his neck glowed. Her brush poised, Andrea heard the censure in his voice.

'It's on too small a scale,' he said. 'Too trivial.'

The hurt that shot through her tightened her lips, but before she could say anything he leaned forward and picked up the painting, holding it carefully so that the paint shouldn't run.

'This is too much on the surface of things.'

He spoke in such a calm, matter-of-fact way that he might have merely been making polite small talk.

'It's flat and uninteresting.'

Speechless, she watched him replace the painting on the ground at her feet. Then she sprang up.

'How dare you!' she cried, swallowing back tears of humiliation. Couldn't he see he was squeezing the very life blood out of her? She grabbed frantically at her paints and thrust them in her bag.

'Go,' she said. 'I didn't ask for your opinion. Just go and leave me alone.'

He got up and stood looking at her with a serious expression in his blue eyes.

'My dear Andrea, you're capable of much more depth than this.'

She heard a huskiness in his voice that hadn't been there before. He waved his hand at the beck and the trees beyond.

'These subjects are too light, too pleasant for your talent. I'll show you things deep in the earth that will change your whole

69

outlook.'

He seemed not to notice that he had upset her deeply, and his indifference was a sword-jab.

'Come with me when we next go caving;' he said, completely unaware. 'It's fascinating.'

She took a deep breath, struggling to keep calm.

'Please leave me alone.'

He looked up at the trees on the other side of the beck with his eyes half-closed. Another gruesome activity being planned, she thought bitterly as she hurled her painting water into the bracken. Did he never rest? He seemed to make up his mind suddenly, and was off before she could say any more.

The evening, workwise, was in shatters. Why couldn't he stay away from her? He had no conception of how others felt, and cared even less. She smoothed her hair back, and bent to pick up her painting with shaking hands. She sank down on a lichened rock for a moment, concentrating on controlling their trembling. Then, getting up, she slung her bag on her shoulder and held her painting carefully in front of her as she walked through the bracken.

There was a lump of pain in her chest and the soft, evening air only intensified it. The fells had a beauty all their own in this gradually dimming light, a beauty she wanted to catch for ever. And she would, in spite of

Tom's censure. She would please herself what she painted. There was no way he could organise her as he planned to do with the house and the cottage, too, if someone didn't stop him.

Andrea heard the notes of the piano as she came down the hill and into the garden. Great crashing chords filled the air, and sent a shiver of dismay through her. Obviously her sister had returned, but why the thunderous playing? She entered the house through the open french windows, and stood for a moment, unseen.

Nadine was seated at the piano attacking the instrument as if it had done her a great wrong. Her back was ramrod-straight as her hands crashed down on the keys. Then she stopped with a suddenness that was shocking. Andrea listened guiltily to the echo of the fading notes, aware that it was her entry that had stemmed the flow. Her sister spun round on the piano stool. Her face was pale and she bit her lip as she stared at Andrea who came farther into the room.

'I didn't know you were back, Nadine,' Andrea said, feeling at a disadvantage, as if she should have been waiting at home to greet her.

'Where have you been for the last two nights?' Nadine asked sharply. 'No-one tells me anything.'

'When did you arrive, Nadine?' Andrea

asked as pleasantly as she could. 'Have you eaten? I only got back myself from London about five o'clock. Since then I've been working on this.'

She placed her bag on the floor and held out her painting towards her sister. Nadine glanced at it and shrugged her shoulders.

'Have you seen Tom?'

Andrea's lips tightened.

'Only briefly.'

Andrea picked up her bag, intending to escape to her room before he appeared, but Nadine motioned her back, and stood up. Andrea could see now that she was looking very tired, and that the tiny lines round her mouth had deepened a little.

'About the house,' Nadine said. 'I intend . . .'

The sound of the telephone in the hall cut her short, and she stood poised with her head to one side. It stopped ringing, and Andrea knew that Tom must have answered it. The deep silence in the room as they awaited was overpowering. Andrea wanted to leave but the call might well be for her. Nadine appeared to think the same because she walked towards the door, and met Tom in the open doorway. The expression on his face halted her.

'What's the matter?' she said sharply, walking back a few steps. 'The concert in Birmingham?'

'Not that. If only it had been.'

As if in a dream Andrea watched him coming towards her. She gazed up at him as he took her painting from her and placed it on the piano top. He seemed to be taking infinite pains not to harm it which was strange after his cruel rejection of her work only a short time ago. She looked at him wonderingly, unable to understand the change in him.

'Sit down, Andrea,' he said.

He caught hold of her arm and propelled her towards the sofa. Seating himself beside her, he leaned towards her solicitously. Before he could say anything, Nadine spoke sharply.

'What's the mystery? Has someone died?'

He hesitated for a moment.

'I'm afraid so.'

He glanced up at Nadine, and then turned to Andrea again.

'My dear, I have bad news.'

'Stephen?' she asked through dry lips.

He nodded.

'Quite suddenly, on Monday. A heart attack.'

She stared at him blankly.

'But . . . but he can't have!'

'His solicitor has been trying to contact you.'

She clutched the arm of the sofa.

'But I've been down in London, and I didn't know.'

Mumbling she looked from one to the other.

'The funeral?'

There was deep compassion in Tom's eyes.

'Today.'

'Why didn't they tell me?'

She tried to stand up, but the room was spinning. She felt strong arms about her as she sank down again and leaned against Tom's shoulder, glad of his support.

'In the end, the solicitor was able to find Sarah's phone number and she told him you were here,' he said as he gently brushed her hair away from her forehead.

She moved slightly, struggling through a mist of unreality to concentrate on Tom's deep voice. It seemed to be coming to her in waves.

'He discovered the connection with Silvergarth House only today,' he said, clasping her shoulder more firmly. 'There was no-one in earlier. He was relieved to get through now.'

She felt Nadine move towards her, and looked up to see a hard expression in her sister's eyes.

'My sympathies,' Nadine said. 'I suppose it's a shock.'

She straightened her shoulders, and threw a disdainful look at Andrea. The look she then flicked at Tom was searing.

'Life has to go on,' she said coldly.

He said nothing. Andrea, though conscious of the warmth of his hand on her arm, felt

74

frozen in space. She couldn't think, couldn't take in what Tom had told her. Nadine moved across the room to the piano, and then back again. This time her eyes brightened as she looked down at her sister as if she had just thought of something beneficial.

'It's hopeful for you, Andrea, that the solicitor's anxious to get in touch.'

Andrea looked up at her blankly while Tom shot her sister a warning glance. Nadine turned away and perched on the arm of a chair as he removed his arm from Andrea's shoulders and stood up.

'A drink, I think.'

He moved towards the drinks cabinet, and poured three measures of brandy.

'I knew Stephen wasn't well,' Andrea said as she accepted one with trembling hands and raised it to her lips.

As the fiery liquid stung her throat she remembered Stephen's wan looks on their visit to the Rocks, and his attack that left him white and breathless. He had enjoyed the visit so much, wanting to return for a whole day's work there. Now it was not to be. If only she could have made him really happy.

'Are you all right?' Tom's voice sounded at her side.

She gazed at him through a haze, seeing only Stephen's pale face.

'When did you last eat, Andrea?' he asked kindly.

She shook her head.

'I'm not hungry.'

'Food.'

He looked towards Nadine's unresponsive back and then sprang up.

'Let's hope I can find something.'

Nadine rose and moved to the piano as he left the room. She sat with her hands running lightly over the keys. Gradually her playing became more sombre until she was bringing her hands down hard in great, forceful chords that gradually slowed into something resembling a funeral march. The next moment the door burst open and Tom erupted into the room. Andrea felt his anger like a living thing.

'Stop it, Nadine!' he ordered. 'Have you no sense, no feelings?'

She glared at him, her hands frozen on the keys. For a moment Andrea thought he would strike her. Instead he pushed her hands aside and snapped shut the piano lid. The sound echoed in the room like a pistol shot. Nadine got up from the piano stool and walked to the window. With her back to them she spoke coldly.

'Too much fuss, Tom. I don't like it.'

He took a deep breath, visibly gaining command of himself.

'I've made sandwiches, Andrea, and coffee. In here, or the kitchen?'

'The kitchen, please.'

He had arranged cheese and salad

76

sandwiches on a round tray that looked ready for carrying into the sitting-room, but she would have choked in there, Andrea thought as she sat down on a stool at the kitchen table and started to eat. She hadn't realised how hungry she was. Tom stood watching her in silence.

She felt the colour flow back into her cheeks as she finished.

'That's better,' he said in satisfaction. 'The solicitor wants you to telephone him at the office tomorrow. Mr Alderburn of Niddle and Alderburn. The number's on the pad.'

She stood up quickly, and the room spun. Tom sprang forward and caught her in his arms. She leaned against him, taking deep breaths, making no attempt to move. He seemed content to stay that way.

'Will they know what happened, and where?' she asked at last. 'You see, Stephen had no close relatives, and . . .'

She broke off, guilty tears stinging her throat. Stephen had been so lonely, and she had done nothing to help. Tom moved slightly and held her more tightly against him. The warmth from his body was comforting.

'They'll know, Andrea,' he murmured. 'Someone will tell you.'

'I should have been with him, gone back to London with him. He'd been ill you see, and . . .'

'Don't blame yourself, Andrea. Nothing

would have changed.'

She took another deep breath, knowing he spoke the truth. Yet her heart told her she should have been kinder to Stephen before it was too late, and she could hardly bear it.

At last she moved. Tom let her go, a gentle expression in his eyes as he smiled down at her. They heard the piano again as they went into the hall, but this time Nadine's touch was delicate. They paused for a moment, listening, Tom's hand on Andrea's arm. He opened the door into the sitting-room as Andrea moved towards the phone. The door closed behind him, and the piano was silent.

Feeling suddenly bereft, Andrea gazed at the closed door. The quietness was unnerving, and her strange sense of rejection was hurtful. She had known he would return to Nadine, but it made no difference. Slowly she went upstairs to her room, forgetting she'd been going to use the phone.

It was late when she thought of Sarah who probably didn't yet know about Stephen. How could she have forgotten? It was too late to telephone now, but she would do it as soon as she was sure Sarah would be up in the morning. She had been kind to Stephen and made him welcome at the cottage for the time he had been here. He had been happy there.

Andrea rose early and showered. Her towelling robe felt damp against her body as she went swiftly downstairs to the hall to pick up the phone and dial the number of the cottage. Sarah's deep Yorkshire voice brought tears to Andrea's eyes.

'You don't sound like yourself, lass.'

'It's Stephen,' Andrea said with a catch in her breath. 'There's bad news, I'm afraid. He died suddenly last Monday of a heart attack.'

There was a long pause on the other end of the line, and then a torrent of sympathy that was almost more than she could bear.

'Can I come and see you, Sarah? I'll be right over.'

Andrea's hand shook as she replaced the receiver.

Once dressed she headed straight for the cottage where Sarah was waiting for her. As soon as she opened the cottage door the older woman enveloped her in a huge hug.

'Come on in, lass. I've got tea made, and toast. You look as if you need something inside you.'

They sat at the table while Sarah plied Andrea with food, talking all the time about how grand a lad Stephen was and how she had liked spoiling him for the time he was with her.

'He said it was the happiest time he'd had for ages,' she said proudly. 'Ah, poor lad.'

They sat in companionable silence for some time and then Andrea got up to go, promising to come back to see Sarah soon. She paused in the doorway.

'I heard a rumour that you're thinking of moving. Tell me it's not true.'

'Nay lass, there's no truth in that. Where would I go? I get lonely here sometimes but I'll not be leaving.'

Andrea smiled.

'That's what I wanted to hear, Sarah.'

With her mind on Stephen, she walked back to Silvergarth. She would phone the solicitor as soon as she got in.

*   *   *

'Mr Alderburn is on his way now to see you,' she was told as soon as she got through to the solicitor's office.

'He is?' she said in surprise.

'He had clients to see yesterday in Bradford and stayed overnight. He should be with you in half an hour.'

She flew upstairs to change out of her old jeans. There was no sound from either Tom or Nadine as she then prepared a tray in the kitchen and saw to it that the coffee was ready for the arrival of the man who had been Stephen's solicitor and family friend.

CHAPTER SEVEN

When at last the solicitor, Mr Alderburn, left, Andrea went through the open french windows into the garden, glad that she had met the man who had watched Stephen grow up and was so fond of him. She was glad, too, that she had suggested he keep Stephen's latest portfolio of work as a memento of the young man he had come to regard almost as a son.

Her sandalled feet were wet as she walked on the grass. She took deep breaths of scent from the roses, remembering Stephen's love for them and his joy when he'd discovered an early rosebud in Sarah's tangled garden. She was still unable to take in fully the implications of the news Mr Alderburn had come to tell her.

Now her tears mingled with the cool dewdrops as she broke off a rose to hold it to her face, savouring its perfect beauty. The pink of each petal deepened at the centre, and tiny lines of colour ran to the slightly-curled edges. Deep inside her she felt a stirring of desire to capture its perfection in the way she knew best. Behind her she heard steps on the gravel, and turned to see Tom.

'I was looking for you, Andrea,' he said, his voice gentle.

She walked towards him, the rose still in her hand and a smile trembling on her lips. For a moment he stood still, gazing at her. She was unable to read the expression in his eyes, but it seemed to her that the tension between them had eased since she had heard of Stephen's death.

He smiled.

'I shall be going out presently while Nadine has a practice session. I'm taking the group to York today. Would you care to join us?'

She saw now that he was wearing pale jeans and a cream shirt instead of his usual outdoor gear. She shook her head.

'I think I need to be alone,' she said. 'I need to think. There are things I need to do . . . commissions from the gallery . . . I think it's best.'

He nodded. She was grateful he made no illusion to the meeting with the solicitor.

'Good idea. Keep yourself busy. Come with us another day. I'd like you to see some of our activities.'

'Yes,' she said. 'Perhaps.'

As she returned to her room to change her clothes once more she remembered her water colour of the beck she had been doing yesterday and which Tom had disliked so much. He had put it down on the piano. She went to find it on her way out, but it was no longer where she had left it. She looked down at the waste-paper basket, and there was the painting screwed up into a ball!

She picked it out and smoothed it as well as she could. Someone had made a good job of destroying it. Nadine? Not that it mattered. She had wanted to destroy it herself because it had been painted on the day she had learned of Stephen's death. It seemed to her that it was the right thing to do in Stephen's memory. She screwed it up again and tossed it into the basket.

The following morning Andrea still found it difficult to concentrate but decided she must make the effort. She decided she would stay in the garden today, well out of Nadine's way, and start one of her delicate flower paintings. The roses were beautiful and the creamy pink one over by the wall would be a good subject to start with.

Silver accompanied her outside when she had collected her paints and paper and the board to rest on. She was glad of the kitten's company until he grew tired of staying in one place and went off exploring among the bushes in the other corner of the garden.

She settled down to work, but nothing seemed to go right. Her gift for capturing the moment seemed to have left her. She tried again on another sheet of paper with slightly better results, but her interest wasn't really in it. The vision of Stephen as she had last seen him seated on the garden wall at the cottage kept floating into her mind.

It was not until much later that it occurred to her that there might be something worthwhile she could do in Stephen's memory, something big and lasting. Stephen had left her all that he had. When the solicitor had told her this her first bemused thoughts had been that she didn't deserve it, that she couldn't possibly accept it. But he had taken pains to convince her that it had been Stephen's wish. There was no-one else to inherit anyway, and the considerable amount of money must come to her.

Why shouldn't it be used for a memorial to Stephen? She would think of something fitting, something that could benefit other young artists perhaps in a way that Stephen would have appreciated. Suddenly she threw down her brush and sat with her head in her hands. She hadn't cried for Stephen properly before, but now it all came pouring out in a flood of tears she couldn't control. She wouldn't see Stephen again, would never hear him talking of the plans he was making for his life and how he had wanted to include her.

At last her tears subsided, but she still sat there, thinking of his wasted life. He was so young, so vulnerable and there had been no-one close to him except herself and she had failed him badly.

She felt Tom come and stand beside her. He placed his hand on her shoulder, a strangely comforting gesture. She wanted desperately to bury her face in the thick sweater.

'Andrea,' he said gently, 'no good comes of torturing yourself. You're too much alone.'

She raised her face, shaking her loose hair out of her reddened eyes.

'Come out with us today. It will help to take you out of yourself, and you'll be doing us a good turn as well. We need three leaders to accompany the boys and girls or we can't go and we're short.'

He gave her shoulder a slight press, and then removed his hand. The look he gave her was serious.

'Will you come with us?'

Put that way she could hardly refuse. She stood up.

'If you want me to come.'

There was a strange look in his eyes for a moment. Then he smiled.

'I want you, Andrea. I want you to come with us.'

She tried to smile, but it was a weak effort.

'Then, yes, I will.'

'Good girl.'

He moved towards the door.

'They'll all be grateful to you. I'll fill you in on the way.'

She smiled tremulously.

'How long before we go?'

'Say half an hour. Bring plenty of warm clothes.'

There was time for a coffee before she heard the engine of the Land-Rover start up. As she pulled the front door shut behind her, Tom leaped out of the driver's seat to take her bag from her and place it in the back

'We're picking up the gang in Gardingley,' he said as they moved off. 'One of my partners will meet us in the carpark up near the top of Lowesdale. It's Gyte Pot for us all today. Quite exciting.'

'We're going caving?' Andrea exclaimed.

'Why not? You'll love it.'

She wasn't so sure. His voice was full of an easy confidence that sent her spirits plummeting. Suppose she was no earthly use to him at all?

She was silent as Tom stopped the Land-Rover in the carpark in Gardingley. The talk and laughter as everyone piled into the back only made her feel worse. They set off again. There was a distinct ache of fear at the bottom of her stomach when they reached their destination at last.

She didn't know what to expect, certainly not the small, rocky hole at the base of an outcrop of limestone at the bottom of a sloping field. Her horror must have shown on her face for Tom smiled at her reassuringly before introducing her to his young partner.

Anna grinned as she pulled on her wetsuit. Her short straight hair was damp with the drizzle that misted the air.

'Come on, you lot!' she boomed so suddenly that Andrea jumped. 'Get your helmets on and the lights checked.'

They walked down the field on the squelchy grass Tom halted in the entrance of a small, rocky hole at the base of an outcrop of rock and waited for the excited chatter to die away.

'Listen,' he said, his face grave. 'You know the drill. Single file, each one of you keeping a close watch on the one immediately in front and behind you. Understood?'

'Understood,' they chorused.

'Put your lights on now.'

'I go first, Andrea next and the nine of you one after the other. Anna's last. Ready?'

In the cold darkness, Andrea heard the sound of rushing water as she clambered over the boulders, trying to keep up with him. She did her best to keep her head down, but every now and again her helmet crashed against the rock above and echoed so much inside her own head that she wondered Tom didn't hear.

'You can stand upright now,' she heard him say.

She didn't know this herself because her helmet light shone only in front of her. There were murmurs of surprise as the news was passed back down the line. As they moved forward now there was water beneath her feet.

'The river,' Tom's voice came back to her. 'Stand still, Andrea, till everyone's gathered.'

In a silent, wondering group they shone

their lights round the cave when he told them to.

'No living thing exists down here,' he said. 'No natural light to make it grow, you see. No slimy weed on the rocks in the water because without light nothing grows.'

Andrea got herself through the water to be helped up the rocks on the other side by Tom. In her turn she helped the girl, Susie, behind her. Then they went downwards for some way until a wider cavern was reached.

'We're nearing the pool now,' Tom warned. 'It'll be waist deep in parts so take care.'

Andrea heard a gasp from Susie as the message was passed back, and could feel her hesitation.

'Hold my hand,' she said. 'We'll help each other.'

Susie's cold, trembling hand gripping hers tightly made Andrea lose all sense of apprehension herself. Strangely, she was unaware of the coldness of the water.

'I'm out!' Tom called back.

As they stood together on dry land Andrea felt a sense of happiness that wouldn't have seemed possible an hour ago. Down here in this subterranean world she was a different person, physically soaking wet but mentally free of any fear. She smiled at Tom and saw his eyes shine back at her in the lamplight. A warm glow filled her heart, and for a moment it seemed to her that they were alone in a world of their own.

Then the helmet lights made patterns on the rocky roof as they all looked up. Tom shone his own beam downwards, indicating that there was an even steeper downhill bit for them to negotiate.

'The river courses through here in flood in spring and autumn,' he said in a matter-of-fact tone as they moved on. 'We've come to the mud slide now. Watch me as I go first. I'll stand at the bottom and catch you.'

He sat down, and let himself go into the blackness. As he got to his feet, Andrea's light shone on his cheeks. At once she was filled with awareness of him that was like the shock of icy water and a surge of warmth simultaneously.

'Come on,' he said, and smiled so dazzlingly that it seemed to her that a great light lit up the darkness. 'Put your feet there, Andrea. Now!'

The muddy slime bit at her nostrils as she obeyed. She trembled at his nearness, afraid for an instant at being so close to him. She saw the deep cleft in his chin and the lines in his cheeks. She saw the strength in his shoulders as he got into position to help Susie and the others as he had helped her. And all the time she knew a deep delight in the thought that she would go with him trustingly into the very depths of the earth.

The light from her head searched out the

jagged, secret indents in the rocky walls as she waited until they were all to proceed farther down the narrowing passage. The roar of the invisible river was above them now, and she marvelled that the roof could support all that rushing water.

Again they stopped, and Tom counted the helmet lights. As they set off again he shone his light at waist level for Andrea's sake only.

'About thirty passages go off from here,' he said to her quietly. 'Some have fifty-foot drops. They haven't all been explored properly yet.'

She was humbled into silence. Tom pointed upwards, and the light from Andrea's raised helmet picked out a narrow opening high up in an expanse of white rock. He swung himself up to wriggle through head first.

'The calcite bridge,' he told her as she hoisted herself through after him. 'Now for the tunnel, a five-minute crawl.'

'Five-minute crawl,' Andrea called behind her as she got down on her hands and knees.

It wasn't as bad as she had feared because there was space at each side of her as she crawled along. Then they were all through. Now there were more difficulties ahead.

'We've come to the rope bridge,' Tom said. 'Don't panic. It's a metre long, that's all, and I'm here to help you. One step on it, slide your foot along, leave go of the rock and then take my hand.'

She did as he said, glad to obey him and to show him her perfect trust.

'Sit at my side,' his reassuring voice came in the darkness. 'Wriggle yourself along now with your feet on the rock and your knees supporting you.'

It sounded horrific, but there was no escape. Her lamp shone on his face as he gazed up at her.

'All right, Andrea?'

She nodded, and then realised he couldn't see because he had dropped himself down the narrow black fissure at her feet.

'I'm all right,' she told him.

'Good girl.'

His approval warmed her. Her helmet clashed on the rock as she slithered through the crack, too, and was lowered to solid ground. She took a deep breath of relief at having coped so far.

'Wait round the corner,' he said as he prepared to climb back up again 'It'll take some time to get everyone through.'

Andrea found a rock for a seat, conscious she was on her own. In the deep, dark silence it seemed as if all her senses sang.

CHAPTER EIGHT

Time seemed meaningless. It could have been five minutes or five hours later, she didn't know which, when Andrea heard Tom's voice again. There was the thump of something landing heavily and the scrape of boots on rock. Then Susie was beside her, babbling in relief at having got across the rope bridge and down through the rift.

Andrea thought of the cottage and Silvergarth. The problems concerning the properties no longer seemed of importance. Only this mattered, pitting oneself against the forces of nature. When she was with Tom what he wanted she wanted, too. She knew something else with unshakeable certainty. Nadine could have no possible understanding of Tom. His plans and ideas were as much part of him as breathing. She understood this and how they made him the man he was. Nadine didn't, and never would.

The sound of Tom's soothing voice as he guided the last person through the rift came to her. They moved on, a moving necklace of light, until Tom halted as they came to a rushing torrent.

'The river again,' he said. 'The noise we hear is a waterfall round the corner. We'll climb up it in a minute, but first turn off your lights.'

Startled, they did as he said. Andrea's eyes ached as she stared into blackness.

'Nothing in the world is darker than this,' he said.

'Why is this cavern so huge?' Susie asked, her voice awed.

Tom's light flashed on, followed by the others. The faces were white in the sudden illumination. Their utter trust in him brought tears to Andrea's eyes. He must be allowed to continue his fine work, she thought, as she listened to him explaining that this was limestone country and limestone was one of the most soluble rocks which meant that bits broke off and were carried along by underground rivers. She would help him all she could.

'Water only erodes rock when it's charged with fragments because they act as a rasp. It takes thousands of years.'

The cave was illuminated in sudden bursts as heads moved. No-one spoke.

'It's fascinating,' Tom went on, his voice vibrant. 'No-one knows why one cave is so massive or why some passages spiral underneath themselves. It's a unique world down here.'

Clambering up the side of the waterfall was like climbing a waterlogged staircase. At the top Tom turned to help Andrea. His hands were cold but a warm glow went through her.

She didn't want him to let go.

'Thanks, Andrea,' he said, his voice close to her ear. 'You coped brilliantly.'

'It was great,' she whispered.

'You'll come again?'

'I'll come.'

The rest caught up with them and it was time to move off again. Turning the next corner she saw something that quickened her feet.

'Daylight,' she called a tremor in her voice.

'Daylight,' the cry went back behind her.

Andrea recognised the opening as she emerged, blinking, into bright sunlight.

'But we came in this way!'

Tom undid his helmet strap and pulled it off. His eyes laughed down at her. She smiled back, took off her own helmet and shook her hair free. They all looked a filthy motley crew.

Anna had the back of the Land-Rover down by the time Andrea reached it and was handing down rucksacks and dry boots.

'Get changed, everyone, then we'll eat.'

A carefree sense of abandon was in the air. As she finished getting into her dry jersey and jeans Andrea saw Tom among the boys, laughing and joking. For a second their eyes met, Then he looked away and started towelling his hair vigorously. Afterwards they stood together at the back of the Land-Rover waiting for Anna to pass down the food. Andrea raised her eyes but found Tom's gaze difficult to meet.

'Come on,' he said. 'We'll walk to the top. Just the two of us.'

He caught a packet of sandwiches and then another.

'We'll not be long,' he called back.

They set off through the heather, the breeze ruffling Andrea's hair and bringing a glow to her cheeks. Over the brow of the hill he stopped. She turned towards him and was surprised to see an expression of tenderness on his face.

'Andrea,' he said softly, letting the sandwiches fall unheeded to the ground, 'it meant a lot to me having you with us. You seem to understand now the work I'm trying to do.'

'I think it changed me, being down there,' she said quietly.

She seemed caught in something so deep it was unfathomable. Then the moment passed. He moved towards her and took her in his arms. She melted against him. The eggshell blue of the sky seemed to shimmer as his lips pressed hard on hers.

'Andrea,' he whispered, pulling her down beside him on a patch of grass. His arm tightened round her and she felt a glow of happiness that she knew made her eyes sparkle. But something made him pause. She felt a quick, sharp sense of loss. Nothing had changed yet he was pulling back his arm and raising himself on one elbow. Then he sat up. She raised herself and sat gazing down into the next valley with her arms round her knees.

'What's wrong?' she asked.

For answer he sprang up and went striding off down the hillside without a word.

'Tom, wait,' she cried as she followed him.

She arrived at the bottom, out of breath and shaking. Tom, surrounded by a crowd of boys, gave no hint that anything out of the ordinary had occurred.

They'd forgotten their sandwiches, she thought wildly. She felt a flush of anger that Tom should treat her like this. It was clear she would never understand him. She had been foolish to think that she did. Deep underground she had learned something about herself though. She knew she needed to help him at whatever cost to herself.

'Time to go, everyone,' Anna called.

Tom left the group and joined Andrea.

'We'll put your bag in the car. Anna's now taking them abseiling. I'll join them when I've dropped you off at the house.'

He sounded matter-of-fact. Was it possible he didn't know the wound he'd inflicted by his headlong flight down the hill? She could hardly believe it. A deep silence hung between them as they drove to Silvergarth. As they arrived and Andrea got out, hazy sunlight broke through the cloud, highlighting the pink roses against the wall. A bee buzzed among them. Suddenly the sound intensified until it filled the air and overwhelmed her senses. Unaware of what was happening she slid to the ground.

Tom sprang towards her and kneeled to help her into a sitting position.

'Keep still for a moment.'

His tone was brisk.

Leaning against him in glorious agony, she felt the beating of his heart as he began to stroke her hair.

'Like silk,' he whispered.

Gently he eased her away from him, and his warm smile hit her heart. He got to his feet and helped her up, too.

'You've had a bad delayed shock about Stephen's death. It takes some getting used to. This is my fault. I shouldn't have persuaded you to come with us today.'

She tried to tell him that had made no difference but he didn't seem to hear as he unlocked the front door and ushered her inside. She shivered.

'I'm hungry. You must be, too. A hot drink?' she asked.

'Sit down, Andrea. I'll do it.'

He filled the kettle and reached down two mugs from the shelf and found coffee and milk. There were some biscuits and cheese handy, too. Helplessly she sat and watched him.

'You must have cared for Stephen very

deeply,' Tom said as they began to eat

Andrea crumbled the biscuit on her plate.

No, she wanted to cry, it wasn't like that.

But the words stuck in her throat. The nearness of Tom was too much. She had to think to assimilate the happenings of the last few hours and to get them into some sort of perspective.

After Tom had gone, and after dealing with her bag of wet clothes in the kitchen, Andrea went straight up to the room she had set aside for her studio. She was filled with the urge to depict her turmoiled feelings in vivid colour. She trembled with the force of it.

Much later, she stood back from her easel to see the effect she had created using unfamiliar oils. Bemused with her rush of emotion, she gazed at the mass of purples, browns and magentas on the canvas as if someone else had painted them. She picked up her brush again, acutely conscious now of the movements she could hear downstairs that to her sensitive ears sounded like trumpet calls. Tom was back and it was impossible to concentrate because he was so near.

She began to pack up. Then, going downstairs, she stepped outside and listened to the strange, dragging sounds from the side of the house. Investigating, she, found Tom unloading his Land-Rover near the garage door. This stood open ready to receive what looked like mounds of camping gear.

'What are you doing?' she asked.

He turned to face her and she saw the lines of weariness etched deeply at the sides of his mouth. In spite of everything her heart turned over with love for him.

'This is the only place to store it,' he said. 'There's a lot to move and it's getting late.'

'I'll help you,' she said quietly.

He stopped what he was doing in surprise and wiped his hand across his forehead. She stepped forward so he should see she was in earnest.

'I've come to a decision. I agree with the plans you and Nadine have for the house. I'm prepared to let Nadine buy me out.'

He said nothing, but jumped up into the back of the Land-Rover to hand down bundles of equipment to her. He made it look easy but it was all she could do to stagger inside the garage with them. But she wouldn't complain. It was her decision to offer assistance just as it was her decision to help him all she could with the project dear to his heart. There was no going back now.

When at last everything had been stored neatly Tom closed and locked the garage door. Andrea felt drained, physically and emotionally. While the work was being done she was able to control her raging feelings at being close to him. Now it wasn't so easy. He pocketed the key and smiled at her so that for a moment the telltale signs of his own

99

weariness vanished.

'Did I hear you all right a moment ago?' he asked.

'About Silvergarth? I'll tell Nadine. We'll do something about it as soon as we can get together with Martin Ackroyd.'

He smiled again.

'I'm so grateful, but we've got an immediate emergency, Andrea. I've agreed to take a group of youngsters at short notice. I want to integrate them within our existing group and the house is the only place for them to stay, for a few days only, until Saturday. After that I won't move any more in until everything's signed on the bottom line.'

She nodded, and a small muscle moved at the corner of his mouth.

'You understand what I'm saying? We've simply got to use the house.'

She nodded again.

'Nadine's agreeable, of course. And you'll raise no objections to that?'

'I'll raise no objections.'

'Good girl.'

Warmth flowed through her and then faded away again, leaving her by cold. She shivered. She should have felt the same exhilaration as she had felt underground when she had resolved to give him all the help she could. But there was only a bleak nothingness and a wish to get away from him as quickly as possible.

100

She heard Nadine arrive home much later. The sound of low voices on the terrace long after dark kept her awake until the early hours. It still felt wrong that Nadine should be involved in such a venture. What could her sister be gaining from it if it wasn't Tom himself?

She herself would have to move out of Silvergarth. There was no way she could remain while Tom was in residence so now there was another decision to be made. A return to London was the obvious plan. She would have to think about it.

In the days that followed, the colours Andrea used in her painting began to change and she found herself using soft browns and greys now, and silver white like the cascading water in the deep underground falls.

Hidden well away in her studio the morning after her trip underground, she had heard only faintly the sounds of the arrival of the emergency group Tom had told her about. They were using the spare rooms on the floor above. She kept well out of their way, thankful that she took most of her meals with Sarah at the cottage.

For the next day or two she continued to paint in oils. The cold, dark underground scenes she portrayed seemed as natural to her as the rose-scented air she breathed in through the open window, and it helped.

On Saturday, she got out her water colours

again. Now she painted the shadowy, helmeted figures in the glimmer of light on the way out of the black labyrinth and the great burst of sunshine. In it was all Tom's warmth and concern, his drive, his ambition, his vision and courage. Pleased with her work she laid down her brush. She would take it across to the cottage now and show it to Sarah.

She took off her paint-smeared smock and tossed it to one side. In her bedroom she found a clean shirt, tied her hair back and went downstairs with the painting. Mentally she had been so long in her underground world that the sunshine outside seemed too bright. It was like coming to life again. But with it came remembered pain.

To her dismay, Tom's Land-Rover drove towards the front door and stopped. He got out and came towards her.

'May I see?'

He took the watercolour painting from her. His head, bent in concentration, was silhouetted against the sunshine. She braced herself for his harsh criticism, but he looked up and smiled.

'I knew you had it in you, Andrea.'

To her dismay, tears sprang to her eyes. Unwilling to let him see how much his words affected her she turned away.

'This would make a fine illustration for our brochure,' he said. 'Exactly the message I want to get across.'

'Please keep it.'

'You mean it? I'm grateful to you. You have so much talent, Andrea.'

She turned and looked at him. In spite of herself, her love for him welled up in her so that she thought he couldn't fail to see it. She began to tell him—something of her own hopes of providing a suitable memorial to Stephen's talent, something lasting that would benefit others.

'Now I'll be able to make plans,' she said with a catch in her breath.

'Memory is a fine thing. There are feelings, emotions that should never be forgotten.'

There was so much compassion in his eyes that her heart gave a leap. A softness was in the air, a breath of pure magic. She held her breath, not wanting the moment to end. For some reason a vision of a house by the river flicked into her mind. She had noticed a For Sale board in its garden the other day. Was it still on the market?

'I think I've found something actually. It's a house in Gardingley Stephen loved. I could make it a place for young artists. I'll tutor courses, lectures, in his memory.'

Her voice faded away as she thought of the potential that could result from this.

'Thanks for letting our extra children stay here,' he said. 'They've left now. I hope we can meet with your executor soon so we can get going here properly and you can go ahead with your plans, too. Agreed?'

She nodded.

'Have you heard from Nadine? You know about the concert she's giving at Nunham Court this evening? I've a ticket going spare. Will you come?'

Was this a gesture of thanks for her willingness to let Torn and Nadine go ahead with their plans? Keep away from this man, her heart said. She must be left alone to find her own salvation.

'No, no. I can't.'

'Of course, you can, and will. What possible reason have you for missing your sister's recital?'

He saw her hesitation and brushed it aside with a smile so confident she was lost. There was no good reason to refuse to accompany him and of course he knew it, but when he had gone indoors with the painting she was full of dismay. This would be the last time she allowed herself to do anything in Tom's company.

CHAPTER NINE

Andrea decided to wear the clinging white dress she had worn only once before when she had attended the opening of Rupert's gallery.

She couldn't help a small tremor of excitement as she stepped out of the shower and wrapped herself in a huge bath sheet. She slipped the dress over her head, feeling surprisingly glowing and relaxed.

Fastening her gold locket round her neck she paused, wondering why Tom was so anxious for her to accompany him this evening. He never did anything without good reason. So had his plans with Nadine taken a new turn?

Tom seemed taller than ever in his evening suit. The smile he gave her as she seated herself in the Land-Rover warmed her heart.

'You look beautiful,' he said.

Pleasure and shyness mingled in her smile. Previously she had seen him dressed like this for her sister's benefit. Now perhaps it might be partly for her, too. She gave a little sigh, aware of an enigmatic expression in his eyes and a softness about his mouth.

They reached Gardingley and took the main road to Harrogate. All too soon the tyres scrunched over the sweep of gravel in front of Nunham Court. Tom's touch on her bare arm as they walked towards the house made Andrea tremble. She had been here many times when it was open to the public but never on such an occasion as this.

Inside, she was caught up in the excited warmth and anticipation. People stood about in colourful groups and she caught the heady scent of carnations. All these people had paid good money to be here in this magnificent house to hear her sister. Andrea felt suddenly humble.

'What's wrong?' Tom asked.

She smiled.

'It's impressive.'

Many of the seats had already been taken. Tom steered her to the far side of the wide semi-circle of chairs. The room was filling fast now and the lid of the grand piano stood open in readiness. Instruments were being tuned. A mass of bright dahlias illuminated the massive stone fireplace, almost dimming the shaded lights of the lamps that cast warmth on the gilt frames of the pictures on the walls.

Andrea looked at the paintings with pleasure. She remembered from previous visits that most of the great portrait painters were represented here. Tom turned to her, smiling.

'What a moment. I wonder how Nadine is feeling.'

Andrea realised that she was sitting on the edge of her seat with her hands clasped in her lap. She relaxed, smiling, too, as Tom took one of her hands in his for a moment and gave it a little squeeze.

At last the far door opened and the conductor led Nadine into the room. The applause was deafening as she came forward in a crimson dress to seat herself at the piano. Beside her Andrea heard Tom's swift intake of breath. The conductor raised his baton and they began. She had heard her sister play Rachmaninov before but never like this.

When at last it was over she caught Tom's expression of loving tenderness and turned away in anguish knowing it was not for her.

'Shall we go outside?' he murmured.

She followed him through large doors on to the terrace. They stood in silence by the balustrade looking out over the wooded grounds to the lake below. In the dimming light the patches of yellow lichen on the rough stone appeared to catch the last of the sun as it faded behind the trees. Tom put his hands on the wall beside hers, and then covered both her own with a warmth that sent shivers through her. They began to walk to the wide steps that led down to the grass.

Suddenly Tom pulled her round to face him.

'Your eyes are pensive tonight. Did you know your lashes are tipped with gold?'

He bent and kissed her lightly on the lips. Then he folded her in his arms and pressed her hard against him. How many times had she dreamed of being in his arms again, but never had she felt like this. Her cheeks burned with guilt because of Nadine as at last he released her.

'I've never seen you look as beautiful as this,' he said 'You could turn any man's head.'

Then she was in his arms again, and it felt as if she was being transported to regions she never knew existed. Only gradually did she sense that something was wrong in his slight withdrawing from her. When he relinquished her she felt a sharp sense of loss. She saw that his face was pale in the gathering dusk.

'I'm sorry,' he said and it seemed that his words were uttered in pain. There were faint sounds now from the orchestra in the distance. He turned his head to listen.

'Shall we return?'

The inner glow of happiness now seemed dimmed and she wished they had remained inside.

It was Tchaikovsky this time, in a great crescendo of sound. When eventually Nadine finished, the hush was full of deep emotion that erupted into a great roar as the audience rose. Tom's eyes shone.

'Magnificent!'

As the applause died away Tom caught hold of Andrea's arm and propelled her towards an adjoining, book-lined room where drinks were being served. They stood with their glasses in their hands. Through one of the doors in the opposite walls groups of people emerged at intervals. Tom finished his drink and took Andrea's empty wine glass from her. He indicated the open door.

'That's Nadine's reception room. Shall we go in?'

She didn't ask how he knew but followed him through the doorway. A waiter removed a tray from the side table and then withdrew. Nadine stood near a small rosewood table.

'You were superb,' Tom said, taking both Nadine's hands in his.

Andrea smiled.

'Congratulations, Nadine. I've never heard you play as well as you did tonight.'

Looking only at Tom, Nadine gave one of her long, slow smiles. Then she removed her hands from his and picked up her glass of wine. Her eyes glowed as she raised it to her lips.

'So when can we expect you back at Silvergarth? Tomorrow? We have a lot to discuss,' he asked.

Nadine shrugged.

'I'll be in touch.'

To Andrea's surprise, Tom seemed content with this.

'We'll leave you then, Nadine, and give someone else a chance.'

He looked towards the doorway where others were gathered. Relieved, Andrea made to follow him.

'One moment!' Nadine said.

Andrea paused and turned to look at her sister. Nadine's eyes were cold.

'About this scheme of his for Silvergarth, Andrea. Leave Tom Gilmore alone before you burn your fingers.'

Andrea gasped.

'What do you mean?' Andrea asked, astonished at her sister's words.

'You heard me. He'll do anything to get his own way. Has he tried anything on yet or is he biding his time till he gets you home?'

To her horror Andrea felt herself flush. Nadine's eyes glinted.

'Ah, I see he has. He wants something from you, Andrea, and means to get it. That charm is all bluff. He'll suck you dry if you let him.'

'I don't believe you.'

'Please yourself, but don't say I didn't warn you.'

Nadine turned away as other people crowded round. Nothing more could be said now in private.

Outside once more, Andrea found she was shaking and stood still for a moment to calm herself before moving off to find Tom. When she found him she saw he was frowning. Something startled in the look he directed at her caught her unawares. He seemed to be seeing her for the first time. Was he aware of what Nadine had been saying about him?

She was glad he was silent as they got into the Land-Rover and followed another vehicle down the drive. She needed time to come to terms with Nadine's spite, for she was certain that's what it was.

*   *   *

Because of her decision to sell her half of the house, Andrea had been expecting to hear from her aunt's executor, Martin Ackroyd, so when he telephoned next morning she wasn't surprised.

It had been late by the time Tom drew up outside Silvergarth the night before. They had entered the house without a word. He had looked round the hall as if not knowing quite where he was or what he was doing there. Then he wished her a curt good-night and vanished. The purring Silver greeted her when she went into the kitchen. She had picked him up and held him to her cheek.

Now he was purring round her feet as she answered the phone to Martin. He sounded worried.

'It's Nadine again, doing the unexpected,' he said.

'What has she done?' Andrea queried.

'You mean she hasn't told you, Andrea? I'll never understand her, never. Whatever made her go in for it in the first place? A mere whim. And now to cause all this trouble. But she always liked trouble, did Nadine.'

'Martin, what do you mean? What has Nadine said? Tell me.'

'She's pulling out of this adventure base scheme, hers and Gilmore's. She wants nothing more to do with Silvergarth, ever.'

Andrea was silent.

'Andrea, you're still there?'

'I'm here.'

'She's asked me to set up a meeting so that you can agree between the two of you to put the house on the open market.'

'But she can't do it.'

'I'm afraid she can. It was an agreement before your aunt died. You'll have first refusal, of course, but after that . . .'

'But Tom will be forced to give up.'

'She cares nothing for that. Needs the money, she says, for some other project.'

'I must think,' Andrea said rather desperately. 'I've got to work it out.'

'Aye, that's best. There's plenty to think on.'

When he rang off, she stood with the receiver in her hand, staring at it in an effort to understand the workings of Nadine's mind. How could she do such a thing when she knew she would be letting Tom down so badly? With a sigh Andrea replaced the receiver. There was no way she would be able to settle to painting now. Instead she bent to pick up the kitten and went out through the front door to see if Tom's vehicle was still parked outside. It wasn't. Tom had gone off somewhere or other completely unaware of the crisis that faced him!

She crossed the drive to the stone bench against the wall and sat with Silver in her lap, gently stroking the soft grey fur until he made signs of wanting to get down. She let him go, lowering him gently to the ground. He darted after a leaf. She watched him disappear into the bushes, a happy little thing enjoying the present moment.

Sunshine brightened the walls of the house where Tom had dreamed his dreams and must soon relinquish them. Near at hand were tracks and footpaths offering perfect opportunities for outdoor activities. It was Tom's life's work and his only hope had been Nadine. His only hope?

She sat bolt upright, instantly back in her mind at Nunham Court with her sister triumphant.

'That charm, all bluff,' Nadine had said. 'Tom will pretend anything to get what he wants.'

Andrea took a deep, shuddering breath. It wasn't true. How could it be? Tom's compassion after Stephen died had been genuine. There hadn't been a hint of calculation in him either when he persuaded her to go with him to Gyte Pot. Was that where he was today? She leaped up and ran to open the garage doors. Empty —- all the

113

caving equipment gone. So that's where he was! It could be hours before he returned.

For a moment she stood deep in thought remembering the underground river carving its way through the limestone deep in the earth. There was continuity and security in the knowledge that it was forever. There was the thrill of adventure in exploring places no-one had been before. Some of this Tom would convey to the groups in his care. And she could make this possible by becoming his partner.

Fortunately she hadn't yet phoned the estate agent to make an appointment to view the house on the river. She would use her money from Stephen this way instead. Suddenly it was important to see Tom, to tell him that Nadine hadn't been his only hope.

Andrea drove to Gyte Pot as if a demon was after her. She was pleased to see that the Land-Rover was parked in the same lay-by as the other day. She pulled in behind and sat for a moment wondering what she would have done if Tom hadn't been here. Then, reaching inside the glove compartment for her torch, she sprang out and breathed in great lungfuls of fresh moorland air.

She was wearing unsuitable sandals for this kind of terrain and she stumbled over the rocks as she neared the cave entrance to shine her torch inside the passage. How long would it be before the party emerged, blinking, into daylight and Tom would be there with them? Her heart gave an excited leap at the thought of seeing him.

Finding a rock for a seat just outside the entrance, she settled down to wait. When at last she heard voices she thought at first she had imagined them. She got up and went inside. Suddenly the ten members of the group were there, spilling out into the glittering daylight. She was grabbed by a pair of iron hands and propelled to the entrance. The others were halfway up the field, now, whooping in delight.

'Tom,' she cried as he let her go. 'I was waiting for you.'

'Why are you here?'

His eyes were ice-blue, his voice hard.

'I've something to tell you.'

'But why here? Don't you know the danger?'

'I heard you coming. I stepped inside, that's all, only a little way, then waited out here.'

He seemed to relax a little, but his eyes were still hard.

'You have something to tell me? About the house, your sister?'

'You know, don't you?'

He gave a harsh laugh.

'She took pleasure in making sure I knew.'

'But it's all right, Tom. I'll buy Nadine's share.'

'No!'

'You don't understand. I'll be your partner instead of Nadine. You can use Silvergarth as you wish. It's what you want, isn't it?'

'No!'

She stared at him, unable to believe what she was hearing.

'You mean you no longer want the house because Nadine's pulled out of your project? Your work's not important to you any more?'

He set off up the field, and she stumbled along beside him. She swayed a little as they reached the stile and he caught her in the same hard grip as before. She knew it was no good, but she tried again.

'The house can be all yours, Tom. Don't you understand?'

But he didn't answer. She jumped down into the road with legs like jelly and unlocked her car door. Afterwards she had no memory of driving herself back to Silvergarth or of parking the car. Somehow she managed to get herself inside the house and into the kitchen to make coffee, still shocked by Tom's incredible reaction. He had rejected Silvergarth and herself. She cringed now at the way she had laid her feelings bare only to have them spurned.

The hurt gnawed at her. After a while she went into the sitting-room and then back to the kitchen. The coffee cup on the table was empty but she had no memory of drinking from it. Where was Tom now and where would he go? She could no longer stay here. Every moment she would be reminded of the last painful hour and she couldn't bear that. She must make other plans.

There was a mewing outside and she opened the door to let Silver in. Tears filled her eyes as she bent to stroke him.

'You're a true friend,' she told him, picking him up and rubbing his body against her wet face.

Silver's soft purring began to steady her so that after a while she was able to bury some of her agonised hurt. She went upstairs and pulled out her suitcase. Sarah would put her up for a week or so to give her time to view the house down in Gardingley and to make a decision about it. She would phone Martin Ackroyd, too, and find out if he had set up the meeting between herself and Nadine.

That done, there was nothing more to keep her in the North until the purchase of the Gardingley house was complete, and she could set about refurbishing it. She would tutor some of the proposed art courses herself in Stephen's memory, but her base would be in London. The lease on her flat there had months to run. She could take up again the life she had carved out for herself and Rupert would be only too pleased to welcome her back.

CHAPTER TEN

Next morning at Sarah's cottage, Andrea steeled herself to return to Silvergarth. There was packing up to be done, mainly of her painting materials which Sarah had agreed could be stored in the outhouse of her cottage until Andrea was ready to leave. She had phone calls to make, too.

Martin Ackroyd was away for the day so she left a message on his answerphone. But the estate agent had disturbing news. The house Stephen liked had had an offer made on it only the day before. She was welcome to take a look round it if she so desired just in case it wasn't accepted.

So things were moving, and so would she be soon. Silver was no real problem. Sarah, surprisingly, had fallen in love with the little thing. She would be glad to give him a home when Andrea left.

Andrea finished all she needed to do by midday. The car was loaded and ready to be driven round to the cottage. She was just locking the front door when she heard voices and turned to see several members of Tom's group in the drive.

'Tom's not here,' she called to them. 'I thought he was with you.'

She saw that one of them was the girl,

Susie, who had liked her painting. She smiled at her.

'He's gone off on his own,' Susie said. 'Wharfedale or somewhere, a last-minute thing. Anna says it's not like him to let us down. That's why we're here. Anna sent us. She'll be here in the Land-Rover in a minute. It's you we want, Andrea. We need your help.'

'You do?'

Andrea was surprised. She couldn't think what for.

'They won't let us do the gorge run unless we've got three leaders, Anna and Terry and you.'

'But I can't run.'

Susie giggled.

'You don't have to.'

There was the sound of the Land-Rover. It drove through the gateway with Anna at the wheel. She pulled up and stuck her head through the open window,

'All set?'

'She says she can't run,' Susie called to her.

Anna gave a booming laugh. She looked the picture of vitality in her wet suit and with her green woolly hat pulled over her hair.

'Can you swim, Andrea?'

'Yes, but . . .' she began but got no further as Anna interrupted.

'You'll see. Bring waterproofs and warm clothes and your boots. Are you on?'

Andrea nodded.

119

'I'll meet you at the entrance to the gorge. My stuff's at the cottage. I won't be long collecting it.'

'We've got to get going or Tom will be back before we get started.'

'Tom?'

Andrea's heart banged against her rib cage. She was trapped.

'But I thought he wouldn't be here.'

'He's a law unto himself, is Tom. Who knows what he'll do? Everyone in. We're in a hurry.'

Andrea followed the Land-Rover, stopping briefly at the cottage to tell Sarah where she was going and to pick up warm clothes as directed. Her boots were in the car already. She arrived at the entrance to the gorge not long behind the others. Anna was pulling lifejackets out of the back of the Land-Rover and shouting to everyone to get one on.

'You, too, Andrea. Why are you in such a hurry? You're not afraid of Tom, are you?'

Andrea shook her head. She wasn't afraid, merely anxious not to come in contact with him again.

Anna thrust her arms into a lifejacket and pulled on a helmet over her woollen hat.

'Hurry up, you lot,' she bawled.

Andrea sprang to get a lifejacket on quickly. She tucked her jeans into her boots and pulled a helmet firmly down over her head. She was committed now, Tom or no

Tom. Her only hope was to get this over quickly and escape before he joined them. She followed the rest down a steep path to where the river ran over great rocks. Anna's eyes shone with enthusiasm as they walked along until they reached the other end of the gorge.

'We're coming back all the way in the river, scrambling mostly where it's not very deep, a little bit of swimming but not much. It's a lot of fun.'

Sometimes the path was at river level and sometimes it climbed up high above it. They could hear the water all the time as it washed over the boulders in its path. They walked in single file.

'Enjoy yourselves,' Anna said when they had gone far enough. 'It'll be great. Me first, Andrea in the middle and Terry last.'

Laughing, she clambered in and they all followed. The water was icy and Andrea gasped. Whose mad idea was this? She was crazy to be joining in with them. A ribbon of shrieking sound ran all down the gorge, echoing from the steep cliffs on either side. Tom would soon know exactly where they were once he got near. She could think only of Tom and of the hard contours of his face as he refused her offer. Tears filled her eyes as she sprang into the next deep pool behind Susie. She must be away from the gorge before he came. She couldn't bear to see him again.

But as they went, wading and scrambling,

she began to find a strange sense of achievement. The water didn't seem as cold either as she reached for handholds on the rocks where she could. There was something in the rushing water and the knowledge that she was part of the natural world as she followed Susie and was conscious of those following on. She was part of a team just as she had been when they went caving. It was a good feeling.

She was in a deeper, calmer part now for a short while and here it was easier to swim although the water wasn't even up to her waist. When she reached rocks again, the slime made it difficult to scramble out. Luckily her feet located a solid rock and she grabbed at another to steady herself. Then she was in the water again, wading knee-deep in mud.

'I've lost my wellie,' Susie wailed, waving a foot in the air.

Andrea felt in vain for it.

'We'll have to leave it. We're holding everyone up.'

To her dismay the girl burst into tears.

'They'll say I did it deliberately.'

'I'll come back for it,' Andrea promised. 'I promise, Susie. Come on. We'll get left behind.'

To her relief Susie agreed and they set off again over rocks and through pools to a place where trees overhung the gorge and the path was higher up. Then she heard voices and her heart thumped—Anna's booming voice and Tom's deeper one.

'But what's the fuss?' Anna shouted. 'There's no harm done.'

'Andrea's down there?' Tom's incredulous voice came.

'Someone had to do it,' Anna shrieked back at him. 'It's safe enough. She's not made of cottonwool. Anyway, where did you slope off to when we needed you?'

Shaken, Andrea stood still. Then Susie grabbed her hand and pulled her forward through another pool. Tom's anger would be directed at herself once she got out of the river but she didn't know why. What had she done wrong now? They rounded a bend in the river and saw a stretch of calm water ahead. Two massive logs in the water blocked the end of it. As Andrea started to swim behind Susie she was aware of Tom and Anna on the pathway at river level keeping pace with them.

Susie reached the first logs amid Anna's yells of encouragement.

'You've got there, Susie. Well done. Get a grip on one of them and haul yourself out.'

It wasn't as easy as she thought, Andrea found when she got there, too. She stood up in the water to hold the slippery log ready for Susie. The girl stood poised and then jumped into Tom's waiting arms. He passed her along to Anna. Now it was Andrea's turn. Tom turned to her, ready to catch her, too. Taking a deep breath she grabbed the log in an effort to get up on it, but there wasn't anyone to hold it steady for her. She couldn't believe how slippery it was. She wouldn't be beaten. With a superhuman effort she found herself sitting astride it. Then she was up on her feet. One precarious second later she was in Tom's arms on dry ground.

'Well done, Andrea!' Anna shouted.

She struggled free, shaking, her teeth chattering.

'Get changed at once,' Tom ordered.

Susie was hopping on one foot.

'My wellie's stuck in the mud back there. Andrea promised to go back for it.'

'Cut along to the Land-Rover, both of you,' Tom ordered.

'She can't break her promise!'

'Go!'

Andrea clambered into the back of the vehicle behind Susie and pulled down the door. She ripped off her wet clothes, glad of her thick towel and dry things, especially her light sandals after her boots that were heavy with icy water.

'I'll find your boot,' she said wearily.

Emerging, she thrust her wet things into her bag. Susie had finished now and was off to join the others. Andrea towelled her damp hair. She didn't hear Tom approach. So unexpected was the sight of him that she felt it was a trick of vision and that the shimmering air had conjured him out of nothing. She stared at him in silence.

'This lost wellie,' he said abruptly. 'Show me the place.'

She drew her comb through her hair and stuffed the towel in her bag. Leaving it there, she went ahead of him along the path to where it climbed high above the river. The cliff was steep here and the river sounds were muted through the trees. At last she stopped and peered down at the muddy banks of the pool below.

'Here?' he asked.

She nodded.

'But it's too steep to get-down. We'll have to go farther along.'

He removed his watch and handed it to her. Then without a word he let himself over the top, working his way down the side of the gorge through the trees. She leaned over to watch, clutching his watch that felt warm from his arm. A shower of loose rock sprayed beneath him. He paused for a moment, hanging on to the narrow trunk of a silver birch which to her anxious eyes seemed too frail to bear his weight. Then he was off again, his feet slipping from under him.

Unable to watch, Andrea closed her eyes. He gave a shout and she opened them quickly. He had reached the bank and was leaning over to reach down into the muddy pool. 'I've got it!'

She gave an answering shout. He stood upright and held the boot upside down for the muddy water to shoot out. Then he began the upward climb. To her relief, coming up was easier because there were jagged rocks for hand holds that had been no help to him on the descent. Even so, she held her breath as his fair head came slowly up towards her.

'Catch!' he called as he neared the top.

She missed, but the boot landed safely. When at last he stood beside her, she stumbled to her feet. She was still holding his watch and she gave it to him. He strapped it to his wrist, breathing heavily after the exertion. Relieved that he was back safely, she looked at him in silence. The moment seemed to last for ever. She was conscious of the river sound, the trees above them, the smell of leaf mould. It all seemed dark and forbidding.

'Tom,' she said at last.

'You've no business here. It's dangerous.'

'Anna needed me. She asked me to come.'

'She's a fool to get you into this.'

'They couldn't have come without me.'

He glared back at her, his fair head thrown back.

'You're not built for it. You're from a softer world.'

Did he despise her that much that he thought she couldn't cope? She took a deep furious breath.

126

'I'm what?'

'This sort of life isn't for you.'

'How can you say that? What's it got to do with you? Anyway, why should you mind?'

He seemed to grow a few inches.

'Mind? How could I not mind? I go off for a short time and come back to find this.'

'I coped, didn't I? The others managed all right and so did I. Why can't you see that? I want your sort of life, helping these children and giving them something of myself and you're too arrogant to see it.'

She turned to run back along the path. In two strides he was after her, pulling her round to face him and pressing her hard against the wild beating of his heart.

'It terrified me,' he muttered against her hair. 'I thought you'd be afraid of doing the gorge run and I couldn't bear it.'

'I enjoyed it,' she managed to get out. 'I liked the exhilaration of it. Why can't you understand?'

'You enjoyed it?'

He held her away from him and looked at her in wonder. She met his gaze without flinching.

'Nothing can take away from me the joy of doing something I thought impossible. I thought you would have understood that. It was like Gyte Pot. I've changed. My painting's changed. I wanted to help you Tom, but you won't let me.'

She ended with a sob, pulling away from him.

'Andrea,' he shouted after her, 'listen to me.'

She paused and turned round. His expression was softer now.

'You don't know what you're saying, Andrea. You cared so much for Stephen. You're still in shock. You told me about the memorial you wanted to set up in his memory. How could I let you use your money in my project instead?'

All the anger seeped out of her at his words.

'You'd turn your back on all this? You'd go away?' she said in amazement.

'It wouldn't be right however much I wanted it.'

'You tried everything at first to get Silvergarth. Why change now?'

A thought struck her.

'When did Nadine tell you she was pulling out?'

A muscle twitched in his throat.

'You know that. She told you, too, after the recital at Nunham Court.'

'But she didn't tell me, not then.'

Nadine had not mentioned a thing about her intention. She had warned her about Tom, that was all.

'I only knew yesterday. Martin Ackroyd told me. You mean you knew her intentions then and did nothing about it?'

'How could I? Your plans were important to you because of Stephen. I couldn't interfere with that.'

She had to believe him. His sincerity was unmistakable. She looked back at him incredulously. Was it possible that he was risking everything for her sake? Her heart lifted unexpectedly.

'That's why I've been off today,' he said, 'trying to sort something out.'

'And?'

He shook his head.

'Hopeless without capital.'

'I was fond of Stephen, Tom, that's all. He knew that. He accepted that it could never be anything more. I don't have to buy that house as his memorial. I had trouble about accepting the inheritance he left me, that's all. I know he would have wanted me to use it any way I liked, and as soon as I knew about Nadine I came to Gyte Pot to find you but you turned down my offer. You could have had Silvergarth but you turned it down. It's you I love, Tom. It's you who means everything to me. I came to you to help you, but you wouldn't have it.'

He was still for an interminable second. Then he took a step forward and the next moment she was once more in his arms. This time she was folded close to him with a gentleness that was unnerving.

'My dear love. It's you I want, Andrea, more than the house, more than anything. Will you marry me?'

A swift vision struck her, of Tom's tall figure outlined against the sky at Howland Rocks, shouting words of encouragement and herself and Stephen watching him. She recalled the anguish in Stephen's voice as he said how much he envied the sense of belonging the activity gave them. His memorial could be in the continuation of the remarkable work that was Tom's dream.

She blinked up at Tom and smiled. It was like coming out into sunlight after cave blackness.

'Yes, oh, yes, Tom. You'll let me be your partner? I'll buy Nadine's share of the house with the money Stephen left me. That's what I wanted to tell you.'

The touch of his lips on hers was gentle at first and then more demanding.

'We'll see to it that Stephen has a fitting memorial one day, I promise,' he murmured at last, releasing her. 'With you beside me we can do anything.'

His voice deepened with confidence, and Andrea was confident, too. In her mind she could see Silvergarth as a happy base during the summer months for the work Tom wanted to do. In the autumn and spring it would be a perfect venue for struggling young artists as Stephen had once been until his talent brought financial success because he was given the time and opportunity to paint.

Others should have that, too The winter months would be for themselves. Sarah, lonely in her cottage, would be only too pleased to help throughout the year. She would be pleased that at last Andrea was happy and fulfilled in a place she loved and with a man who meant the world to her.

She raised her face as faint sounds disturbed the silence in the far distance.

'Our charges are ready for the off,' Tom said quietly.

She picked up the wellington boot and then gave him a smile of pure brilliance as they set off together—back to the children and to a new future.